Adventure in Paris

Judy Starr

Dolphin Bay Publishing

Adventure in Paris

Published by:
Dolphin Bay Publishing, Inc.
P.O. Box 3664
Dana Point, CA 92629
www.KatieandZackAdventures.com

ISBN 978-0-9899230-4-0
Copyright © 2014 by Judy Starr
Printed in the United States of America
No part of this publication may be reproduced, stored in a retrieval system, or transmitted in any form by any means—electronic, mechanical, digital photocopy, recording, or any other without the prior permission of the author.
All rights reserved solely by the author. The author guarantees all contents are original and do not infringe upon the legal rights of any other person or work. No part of this book may be reproduced in any form without the permission of the author.

Unless indicated otherwise, all Scripture quotations are taken from the Holy Bible, New Living Translation, copyright © 1996, 2004, 2007 by Tyndale House Foundation. Used by permission of Tyndale House Publishers, Inc., Carol Stream, Illinois 60188. All rights reserved.

Scripture quotations taken from the New American Standard Bible®, Copyright © 1960, 1962, 1963, 1968, 1971, 1972, 1973, 1975, 1977, 1995 by The Lockman Foundation.
Used by permission. (www.Lockman.org).

Art © 2014 by Chris Beatrice

Dedication:

To Dad

a gentle and generous man

who gave our family the gift of seeing the world

&

To Frank Marocco

the best jazz accordionist ever, and one of the kindest,

most encouraging people I have ever met,

who gave me a love for the instrument

and showed me what it can *really* sound like.

Chapter 1

"*Ça va? Je peux vous aider?*"

To Katie, the strange, accented voice sounded far away. *I must be dreaming,* she thought, shifting a little on her oddly stiff bed and feeling around for her covers.

The same confusing voice spoke again, only much closer this time. And then something—or some*one*—touched her shoulder!

Katie's eyelids sprang open to find a teenage boy standing over her. She let out a loud shriek, making the boy jump. "What are you doing here?" she gasped, trying to scoot away, only to bump into something hard. Quickly glancing behind her, she discovered the back of a wooden park bench. "Huh—?"

"*Pardonnez-moi!*[1] You speak English," he said in an accent, looking perplexed.

I'm not in Oklahoma anymore! Katie realized in a flash. Looking down, she also discovered with great relief that she was no longer wearing her nightgown, but was now in a pair of white shorts and a bright red top.

Struggling to sit up on the bench, she faced the strange—but very cute—dark-haired teenager standing in front of her. The boy continued watching her with a puzzled expression. Katie tried to brush back her auburn hair, hoping it wasn't a tangled mess, then met his deep brown eyes and said, "Uh…where on earth am I?" And she meant *where on earth* quite literally, figuring she must have been transported someplace far from home…again.

"In Paris,"[2] he stated with a shrug, like of course she should know that.

"Pa-REE?" Katie repeated. Then her mouth dropped open. "Paris?" A slight smile began to grow. "As in France? No way!"

"*Oui, c'est vrai.*"[3] He hesitated. "Where did you think you were?"

"Well…" Katie wasn't sure how to answer that. "Actually… Paris is perfect." *But I might have to pinch myself a few hundred times to believe this!* A huge smile spread across her face.

The teenager took a hesitant step forward and said, "My name is André."[4]

---

1 Pronounced par-dohn-eh-mwah, meaning excuse me
2 Pronounced by the French as Pah-ree
3 Pronounced wee, say vray, meaning yes, it is true
4 Pronounced Ahn-dreh, French for Andrew

She rose to her feet and replied, "Katie."

As her mind grasped this crazy turn of events, she looked around curiously. Behind André stood a tall statue of a man on a rearing horse. To her right, a picturesque arched bridge spanned a wide river.

But what really caught Katie's attention was André himself. His red beret, cocked jauntily on a head of wavy brown hair, matched the red scarf tied around his neck. He wore a black vest over a starched white shirt, and had some sort of big instrument slung across his back. *He looks like a picture from a French magazine,* she thought, guessing he must be about seventeen.

André glanced around. "Are you alone?"

"Um...I'm just waiting," she said, trying to be a bit vague since she didn't know what she was supposed to do. *Mr. Gateman sure didn't give me any warning or instructions this time!* she thought, starting to chew on a fingernail.

"Would you like to wait at our store instead?" he asked, gesturing toward a nearby street. "I believe it is going to rain, and you do not want to be caught out here."

Katie frowned, not quite sure what to do. *Waiting at a store sounds safe enough.* She still had that same dizzying sense as the two previous times when she'd been transported someplace. Only this time Mr. Gateman wasn't around, and she didn't have a clue what to do. *But I sure don't want to get stuck out here in the rain,* she thought, nodding at André with a tentative smile.

André led the way past the huge monument and out through a black metal gate. While they waited at the side of the road for several loud mopeds to whiz past, Katie pointed toward the large black box with white keys slung over his shoulder. "What's that?" she asked over the noise.

André smiled, looking very proud. "My *accordéon*.[5] I play all over Paris, mostly for the tourists, to earn money."

"Oh," Katie nodded, thinking that was a strange activity for a teenager.

"But eventually my father wants me to take over his business," André continued as he motioned for them to cross the street. "He owns Pain de Saint-Louis,[6] and it has been in our family for several generations."

André's voice trailed off, but Katie was too enthralled with the immediate sights of Paris to wonder why.

As they entered the narrow black-topped lane, Katie had to walk behind André on the uneven grey-stone sidewalk, scooting past several pedestrians walking their dogs. Towering above were yellow and white granite buildings three and four stories high, casting a deep shadow on the street.

Katie jumped slightly when church bells began pealing loudly from the cathedral just ahead on the left. A large clock jutted straight out from the church's tall spire, announcing it was one-o'clock. *Just a minute ago, when I went to bed, it was ten P.M.,* she marveled, remembering how time stood still at her house whenever she got transported someplace else.

Thoughts of home brought to mind the unpleasant scenario that had just occurred there. It had only been a few days since

---

5 Pronounced ah-core-deh-ohn, the French pronunciation for accordion

6 Pronounced Pahn deh San-Loo-ee, meaning Bread Store of Saint-Louis

her amazing adventure in the Bahamas with Zack and Danny and the sunken treasure, so she was still feeling restless back home. Unable to sleep, her mom had caught her reading with a flashlight under the covers and had told Katie to turn off the light and go to sleep. About half an hour later, when Katie heard her mom's returning footsteps, she had quickly clicked off the flashlight and acted like she was asleep.

But somehow her mother always seemed to know. "Katie, you've continued reading, haven't you?" she had asked in a stern tone.

Now, Katie felt a pang of guilt, because she had insisted she'd been trying to sleep.

"*Bonjour,* Henri!"[7] Andre's voice interrupted her recollections as he called toward a man in a shop. Katie stopped behind the teenager and glanced through the store window. "Ooo, yuck," she said, wrinkling her nose and pointing at the dead, skinned chickens whose clawed feet stuck straight up in the air. "That's gross."

André looked at her with an odd expression, but didn't reply.

Katie smiled weakly, feeling like maybe she'd said something wrong. But as they moved on, the picture of the chicken claws burned into her memory. *Gives new meaning to "chicken legs,"* she grimaced.

Just as they drew even with the church across the street, the huge wooden doors burst open and people spilled down the steps. Katie watched, wondering why they were at church in the

7 Pronounced Bon-joor, Ehn-ree, meaning "Hello, Henri."

middle of the day. Then she caught her breath.

"Katie!" A short redhead pushed his way between two older French gentlemen and bounded across the street. In his enthusiasm, he practically ran into her. "Am I glad to see you!"

Giggling, Katie gave Zack a gentle slap on the shoulder. "Me too!" she said. "I'm *super* glad you're here!" She glanced toward the church. "But what were you doing in there?"

Zack shrugged. "I guess we never know where Mr. Gateman is going to drop us, huh?" He laughed. "I was just going to bed—" He stopped abruptly when André appeared at Katie's side.

Katie looked up at the teenager. "André, this is my friend Zack. He's the one I was waiting for." She hoped that sounded believable.

André nodded and said, "*Enchanté*,[8] Zack." Katie guessed that meant "nice to meet you."

"And here we are at our store," André motioned just beyond to a shop filled with racks of breads, pastries, miniature pizzas, decorative fruit tarts, and sandwiches. Zack's eyes widened. "Yum!"

Katie leaned toward André. "I wouldn't turn him loose in there, if I were you."

"Hey!" Zack replied. André chuckled.

Before stepping into the shop, however, Katie's attention was diverted by a young French woman bent low just beyond the entrance. She was feeding pieces from a long loaf to an

8 Pronounced on-chahn-tay, meaning enchanted, or nice to meet you

adorable golden retriever. The puppy wolfed down the morsels and looked up with eager black eyes for more.

"He's so cute!" Katie said, kneeling down to stroke its soft yellow fur. The puppy instantly wagged its tail and placed its big front paws on Katie's legs, seeming to grin up at her.

The French woman looked at Katie and said slowly, "I do not speak English well." She rose to her feet, turned toward André, and began chattering away in French while Katie and Zack patted the puppy.

After a few minutes, André looked at Katie and said, "It sounds like this puppy is lost. Mademoiselle told me that she was sitting in front of Notre Dame[9] earlier today,"—he motioned like it was nearby—"and an American family was there with this dog. The husband was tall and thin, with black hair, and he had a pretty wife and a little blonde girl with him. They also had this puppy…but just now she found it wandering around the street here."

"Poor puppy," Zack said.

"Poor little girl!" Katie added, imagining what it would feel like to have lost such a lovable pet. "Do you think we can find the owners?"

André shook his head. "They are tourists. They could be anywhere."

The woman started talking again, and André interpreted once more. "The husband spoke some French, and he asked Mademoiselle for directions, so she thinks their plans are to

9 Pronounced No-trah Dahm, an important cathedral in France's history

visit Notre Dame and the Eiffel Tower on Tuesday, tomorrow, then Versailles[10] on Wednesday. But that is all she remembers. And now she has to go."

Katie scooped the pudgy animal into her arms and stood up. "Well, we can't just leave him," she said, looking at André with big eyes.

André glanced at the puppy, then back toward the woman. He said something in French, and the woman nodded. As she started to leave she said, "*Bonne chance*,"[11] which Katie guessed meant something like "good luck."

The woman vanished around a corner, and André turned and disappeared into the bakery, leaving Katie standing there holding the puppy. *Now what?* she wondered, suddenly feeling lost herself.

Zack looked at the puppy, its tail thumping happily against Katie's arm. "You know," he said, "after eating, that puppy might tinkle on you."

"Yuck!" She immediately set the bundle back on the sidewalk between her feet.

"Uh, Katie," Zack said, "any idea *why* we're in Paris?"

"Uh, Zack," she mimicked, "I went to bed and woke up on a park bench down the street."

He chuckled. "Yeah, I went to bed and woke up in the middle of a Catholic mass. It was pretty interesting…but talk about a weird way to wake up!" Zack flipped his curly hair out of his eyes.

---

10 Pronounced Vehr-sigh, an enormous palace just southwest of Paris

11 Pronounced bun-shawnce, meaning good luck

Katie only gave him a slight smile. Her initial enthusiasm for being in this romantic city had begun to dim in light of having no idea what to do or where to go.

Zack seemed to sense her concern and moved a little closer. With a serious face he said softly, "Did Mr. Gateman give you *any* instructions?"

Katie shook her head.

"So…what do we do?"

"I guess—" She was cut off by the horrific screeching of tires someplace nearby. A split second later Katie realized the puppy was gone!

Chapter 2

"Noooo!" Katie cried, dashing toward the sound as fast as her legs could go. She heard Zack close behind.

In a moment they reached an intersection and found all the cars at a standstill. A policeman in the middle of the traffic jam was bending down to pick up something out of the street. Katie wanted to close her eyes and avoid seeing what she feared most, but her eyes refused to shut.

When the officer stood up, relief flooded over her. A lively puppy squirmed in his arms—but it wasn't *her* puppy. Confusion instantly replaced her relief as she watched the policeman deliver the animal to the opposite sidewalk and scold its stricken-looking owner. *But where did the golden retriever go?*

As she turned around to look at Zack with bewildered eyes, André appeared. "What happened?" he asked, breathless. He no longer wore his accordion.

"Someone almost hit that dog," she motioned across the street. "But it's okay."

"*Très bien*,"[12] he said, obviously meaning "good." He turned and started back toward the bakery.

"But…" Katie trotted after him, feeling foolish at having lost the golden retriever so quickly, "I'm afraid I can't find the other puppy."

To her surprise, André merely gestured for her to follow. As Katie started after him with a heavy heart, Zack came up beside her and whispered, "Aren't we going to look for it?"

At that particular moment, Katie didn't know *what* to do. The puppy was lost, she felt lost….

In a sort of daze, Katie followed André into his bread shop—only to find her puppy happily chowing down the last of a pizza roll.

André smiled. "*You* did not follow me into the store, but the puppy did. It knows where to find food."

Zack chuckled. "My kind of dog."

Katie felt another flood of relief as she picked up the wiggly bundle of joy. "You scared me to death!" she playfully scolded the puppy, looking into its small black eyes. It responded by slathering her nose with a pink tongue.

They all laughed, and Katie set the animal down to finish its snack.

Just then, a door in the back wall opened, and a barrel-chested

---

12 Pronounced tray bee-yen, meaning very good

man wearing a starched white apron emerged. He surveyed the scene before him, then began talking to André in rapid French. Katie couldn't tell if he was upset, angry, or just confused. Her concern grew as he withdrew a piece of paper from his pocket, showed it to André, then began waving toward Zack and her and pointing at the puppy.

Finally André turned to Katie and Zack. "My father wants to know how I met you."

"Oh," was all Katie could think of to say.

"He finds all of this—how do you say?—amazing, because a very large man just came into the store half an hour ago and told my father to watch for an American girl and boy with a puppy."

"What?" Zack said from beside Katie, his mouth dropping open.

Slowly Katie began to smile. This situation clearly reminded her of someone—their special messenger from God! *This sounds just like him,* she thought, the grin spreading across her face.

"*Oui, oui,* it is very…*incroyable,*"[13] André said, looking surprised himself. "The man even made some arrangements with my father, and gave him a note for you, Katie." André took the piece of paper from his father and handed it to the girl.

Katie unfolded the note and slowly read out loud:

"My dearest Katie, welcome to Paris! Your job here is bigger than you think. And this is a perfect place for you to learn something

---

13 Pronounced een-croy-ahb-lah, meaning incredible

very important about yourself, as well as something about your relationship with your Father that will transform you. I have arranged for you and Zack to stay with Monsieur and Madame Boulanger[14] while their daughter Émilie is away with friends. Enjoy Paris, and. . ."

Katie frowned at something on the page and stopped reading. "What does a-muss-eez-vows mean?" she asked, trying to sound out the French words.

"*Amusez-vous,*"[15] André corrected with a smile. Katie could tell he was trying not to laugh. "It means 'have fun'."

"Oh," Katie said, meeting the boy's deep brown eyes. She then looked back down at the note. *I wonder what my big job is and what I'm supposed to learn. And this thing about my relationship with my father doesn't make any sense—he's in Oklahoma!* She shook her head slightly, stuffed Mr. Gateman's note into her pocket, and looked up at André again. "Who are these people we're supposed to stay with?"

"Monsieur and Madame Boulanger are my father and mother," André said, glancing over at the stern-looking man beside him. "We live above the shop." He pointed at the ceiling as if she could see their apartment through the roof.

Katie met Monsieur Boulanger's stare and swallowed hard. *Stay with him? What was Mr. Gateman thinking?* Then she looked

14 Pronounced Mon-soor and Ma-dam, French for Mr. and Mrs., and their last name is Boo-lan-jhey, meaning Baker

15 Pronounced ah-mew-zeh-voo

over at André. *Of course, I don't mind being around André more….*

Monsieur Boulanger interrupted her thoughts, waving his hand toward Katie. "You stay five days. Émilie return then," he said in a loud, heavily accented voice.

She could barely understand the man, and turned concerned eyes toward André. The teenager seemed to read her expression and gave her a gentle smile. "Papa means it is all worked out so you can stay in my older sister's room. It is only for five days because that is when Émilie returns from visiting friends. And she is allergic to dogs and cats." He paused, adding, "Oh, and Zack, you will be sleeping in my room."

"Great," Zack said.

Katie glanced at the boy and smiled to herself. *He's just happy to be living above food.*

Right then the puppy gave a piercing bark. "André?" Katie asked, looking down at the dog, "does your father have any idea who might own this puppy? Did an American family—a man, wife, and little girl—come into the bakery by any chance?"

André spoke briefly with his father in French, then said, "Papa has not seen anyone like that. He said you can look for the owners, but if you have not found them by Friday, the puppy will have to go to"—André's voice abruptly dropped low—"the refuge."

Katie frowned. "The refuge?"

"It is the place for unwanted animals," André replied softly.

"The *pound?*" Zack said with alarm.

Katie's heart leaped. She wanted to ask how anyone could even *think* of sending such a cute puppy to the pound, but when she glanced at Monsieur Boulanger, she was pretty sure people didn't argue with him.

André bent down behind the counter and slung the accordion over his shoulder. "I will take you upstairs now to meet Maman," he said, motioning for Katie and Zack to follow.

Picking up the puppy, Katie carried it past a frowning Monsieur Boulanger as she and Zack trailed André through the bakery. Passing cooking utensils, pots and pans, piles of dough, and warm ovens, the room filled their senses with a heavenly aroma. The puppy's nose sniffed and twitched as he stretched to reach each fresh temptation.

Zack looked at Katie. "I read that a dog's nose is a thousand times more sensitive than ours," he said, reaching back to run a hand over the puppy's head. "This must be driving him crazy!"

They began climbing a narrow, winding staircase in the far corner of the kitchen, the worn wooden steps groaning with each footfall. *No sneaking up and down these!*

André said over his shoulder, "Papa does not speak English much, but Maman taught English before they married. So I grew up speaking English with her—except when Papa was around."

I think I'll just steer clear of Monsieur Boulanger, Katie decided as she followed André into a pleasant dining room on the first level up.

Warm, humid air flowed through a window beside an oval, dark wood table. Just beyond, Katie noticed a white- and blue-tiled kitchen behind a half wall. To her right, a large red tapestry covered a wood-paneled partition, and Katie guessed that a living room must be on the other side. A trim woman with short brown hair and glasses appeared from around the wall, wearing an orange and white apron. She smiled warmly and said in a lilting, musical voice, "*Bonjour, bonjour*. You must be Katie and Zack. We were told you were coming."

"Yes, ma'am," they replied in unison. Katie gave an internal sigh of relief. *At least* ***she*** *seems happy we're here.*

"*Très bien*," she said, reaching out to touch the side of Katie's face with her palm. "I am Monique Brineaux[16] Boulanger." She then took the puppy's face and turned it up toward hers. "And who is our friend?" The animal wagged energetically.

"It's a lost puppy," Katie answered, "but we don't know its name."

"No?" Madame Boulanger said. "But here is a tag." Sliding the puppy's collar around, a small silver tag in the shape of a dog bone caught the light.

"Wow, we didn't even see it!" Zack said, moving closer. "Does it give the owner's name?"

Madame Boulanger bent down and inspected both sides closely, then stood straight again. "No, only the dog's name."

"Really?" Katie said. "What's its name?"

"It says But-ter-ball," she replied, sounding it out slowly. She seemed a bit puzzled.

"Hello, Butterball," Katie repeated, bending her face close to the puppy's.

Responding to its name, the bundle of fur wagged its tail

16 Pronounced Moh-neek Bree-no

and again caught Katie's nose with its wet tongue.

"But *Butterball—*" Katie paused to try and wipe her face against her shoulder, "could be a boy or a girl. I wonder which it is?"

"That's easy," Zack said. In a single movement he scooped the puppy from Katie's arms and rolled it on its back. "She's a girl," he announced, holding the puppy like a newborn. Then he met Katie's surprised eyes. "What? I live on a ranch, for Pete's sake. We have to check animals all the time."

Katie felt her cheeks starting to flush.

Zack rolled his eyes, flipped Butterball back over, and returned the dog to Katie's arms.

Madame Boulanger said, "Well, we will need to fix a litter box for your new friend, *oui?* You know what puppies tend to do." She tussled Butterball's head a little.

"Uh…" Katie said hesitantly, "do you think she could stay with me?"

"*Oui*, but of course," the lady answered. "Your new friend will love to be near you. We will just need to clean Émilie's room before she returns."

"Perfect!" Katie gave Butterball a gentle squeeze.

"*Bien*. Now come. I will show you to your rooms."

Katie, Zack, and André followed the lady up the next flight of stairs, then turned right into a hallway. They first passed a set of double doors on their left, opened to the master bedroom. Katie peeked in and saw a light-filled room with a large poster bed and framed pictures of old people hanging from the white walls.

The hall continued straight into a room that was obviously André's. Photos of accordionists adorned every bright blue wall. A heavy wood wardrobe stood beside the door, and bunk beds pressed against the far right wall. A brown chest of drawers with a large mirror sat opposite. Straight ahead, André's desk and chair rested below a wide open window. Blue drapes fluttered into the room, and Katie surmised from the traffic sounds that the window opened to the street below.

Something looking like a large, battered suitcase rested near the doorway. André stepped around the group and swung his accordion off his back, setting it near the box. "The most important thing in my room," he said as he opened the case and stowed the instrument. "You will be here with me, Zack, in the upper bed."

"Great," Zack said, moving past André into the small space.

"Come, Katie," Madame Boulanger said cheerfully, turning left and leading Katie past a small bathroom. As they started by, Katie saw some sort of small, square-shaped mechanical device to the right of the doorway. *The washing machine?* she guessed. Beyond it stood a single sink and a large gilded mirror. An oversized towel rack hung from the left wall, and in the far corner, next to the toilet, stood a tall, thin glass box. The moment she realized what it was, Katie's eyes grew big. *That's got to be the world's smallest shower!* She shook her head slightly. *This will be interesting.*

When they reached the last room on the right, Madame Boulanger motioned toward the various pictures of French celebrities covering the walls. "You can see that Émilie likes the boys," she said with a shrug. "She is eighteen, a year older than André…so what can we do?"

The room looked a lot like André's, except flipped. And instead of bunk beds, a double bed filled the left corner. Katie stepped in, feeling a bit out of place…until her eyes landed on a green duffle bag beside the bed. *The same bag of clothes Mr. Gateman sent to the Bahamas,* she thought, remembering their recent time in the islands.

Butterball's squirming diverted Katie's attention. "Okay girl, here you go," she said, setting the puppy on the thin red rug covering most of Émilie's wood floor. Finally free, the puppy made a beeline for the desk at the far end, then sniffed along the chest of drawers and over to the wardrobe before flopping down on her side as if exhausted.

"*Oui*, I will go find a box," Madame Boulanger said quickly, turning and disappearing from view.

Now that she was alone, Katie realized how tense she had been as she plopped down on the bed near the duffle bag. But before she could look inside, a voice said, "Are my clothes in there too?"

Katie looked up with a smile, glad to finally have a private moment to talk with Zack. She exhaled loudly. "I'm so glad you're here, Zack."

A curious expression came over his face, then he broke into a grin, making the freckles meld together across his nose. "Hey, this will be fun!" he said, spreading his arms wide. "We're in a new country and everything. Another incredible adventure!"

His constant enthusiasm was exactly what she needed.

"So…are my clothes in there, or what?" he asked again.

Katie slid the zipper open and pulled out a pile of her tops and shorts, then said, "Yup, they're here, along with some funny-looking money." She smiled. "Mr. Gateman thinks of everything."

Zack sat down on the bed, and for the next few minutes they caught up on what had happened since they'd been back from the Bahamas. Talking softly, he told her about discovering how time had stood still at home while they'd been on Elbow Cay. And she told him about the seashell she'd been able to bring back. She didn't, however, mention what she had learned about forgiveness, because she felt pretty sure she would have to practice that again.

Thinking of what she had learned in the Bahamas reminded her of the paper Monsieur Boulanger had just given her. Katie pulled Mr. Gateman's note from her pocket and shook her head. "Now we're in Paris—but I sure don't get these instructions. What do you think Mr. Gateman means by 'your job here is bigger than you think'?" she asked, her eyebrows scrunching together.

"Who knows," Zack shrugged. "Maybe you're going to keep the Eiffel Tower from getting blown up, or something."

Katie gave him a look. *Only a boy would think of that.* She turned back to the note again. "And I'm supposed to learn something important about myself and about my relationship with my father that will transform me. What does *that* mean?"

Before Zack could respond, André's face appeared at the doorway. "Will this be okay?" he asked, motioning around the room.

Katie smiled. "This is great."

"*Très bien,*" André said, then hesitated. "Katie," he spoke slowly as he stepped into the room, "Papa may seem…" André searched for the right word, "…hard. But he is a good man of principle."

When André paused, Katie said, "But would he really send Butterball to the *pound?*"

André dropped his head and stared at the floor for a moment. Finally looking up, he said, "Because of Émilie's allergies, we cannot keep the puppy. So you have until Friday to find the dog's owners."

"But someone could adopt Butterball from the pound, right?" Zack asked.

André looked out the window. "Possibly," he said. "Unfortunately, most French people only want small dogs."

"So what would happen to Butterball?" Katie said in a strained voice.

Slowly André turned to meet her eyes—and Katie caught her breath. She could tell the answer wasn't good.

André glanced at the sleeping animal then looked up, his eyes boring into hers. "Katie, you *must* find the owners of this puppy."

Chapter 3

At hearing the urgency in André's voice, Katie bit her lip and wondered, *But how?* She looked down at the adorable yellow creature sound asleep a few feet away. *Maybe Butterball is my important job...except I don't have a clue what to do.*

Zack looked at André and said, "If we can't find the family and she goes to the pound, how long will she have?"

André shook his head. "It varies, but the shelters around here are so overcrowded that they don't keep animals very long." He glanced at Katie and seemed to read her mind. "But I will help you look for the puppy's owners."

"Really?" Katie brightened slightly.

"*Oui*," he nodded. "I can play my *accordéon* and attract attention. Maybe we will find the American family."

"That would be great," Katie said, happy to have some sort of plan.

André looked down at Butterball. "The woman we met told me that the little girl kept hugging the puppy, because it had been a gift from her grandmother right before the woman died. The child really loved her grandmother…so it is a very special dog."

"Then we've *got* to find them," Katie stated emphatically. "Let's go!"

"Um…" Zack raised his hand slightly, "when do we eat lunch?"

Katie jabbed him in the ribs.

"Well I'm hungry!" he scowled at her.

André smiled. "We own a bakery, Zack. Food is always available." He motioned for them to follow him.

"Yes!" Zack jumped up from the bed.

After they had eaten ham sandwiches on bread fresh from the oven, André stepped outside and declared that the clouds had passed. He decided they should look for the family around the immediate area today, then tomorrow take his accordion to Notre Dame and the Eiffel Tower where the puppy's owners should be visiting.

With Butterball trotting along on a homemade rope leash, the group headed out the kitchen's back door into a central courtyard. A narrow passageway between the bakery and the shop next door led them out to the street again, which was now bustling with locals and tourists.

It soon became apparent that if Butterball's family was

nearby, they would certainly notice the puppy. With her short legs and pudgy body, she would waddle ahead to eagerly sniff something interesting, then unexpectedly flop down in the middle of the narrow sidewalk and refuse to budge. The next instant she would bounce up like a spring and dart to the end of her rope, only to plop down again like a lead weight.

As they walked, André explained that they were actually on an island in the middle of the Seine[17] River. "This island is called Île Saint-Louis,"[18] he said. "And the next island just beyond is called Île de la Cité,[19] where Paris began."

"Paris started on an island?" Zack said, moving up beside André.

Katie sighed. *History again. Well, maybe this will turn out to be interesting, like the pirate stuff in the Abaco Islands.*

André continued. "Paris started small, but grew over the centuries with France's various rulers. Then when Louis the Fourteenth became King in 1643, Paris really expanded. This island we are on became the residence for aristocrats—the very wealthy."

Flipping her hair back, Katie grinned and said, "Oo la la."

Zack ignored her. "So this is the expensive part of Paris?"

"*All* of Paris is expensive now," André smiled, "but by the time Louis the *Sixteenth* and Marie Antoinette came to power, the people revolted because the rulers were living in luxury while they suffered. So the commoners executed the King and

17 Pronounced Sehn

18 Pronounced Ill San-Loo-ee

19 Pronounced Ill deh la See-teh

Queen, along with thousands of others." André made a slashing action across his neck as he looked at Zack and added, "The guillotine was very popular back then."

Katie scrunched up her nose and muttered, "Gross."

"Then came Napoleon," André said. "You have heard of him, *oui?*"

Zack puffed out his chest and acted like he was sticking one hand inside a vest.

"Yes," André chuckled, "that is the way he is always painted. Napoleon helped elevate France to a leading world power. Then after we endured the horrible World Wars, Paris became—" André swept his arm wide, "the most beautiful, romantic city in the world."

Katie smiled at André's obvious love for his city. Looking around, she had to admit—Paris was special. Sidewalk cafés overflowed with smartly dressed Parisians nestled around small round tables, the latest fashions hung from mannequins posed in classy store windows, and tempting chocolates beckoned from decorative displays. The city seemed to radiate energy.

Nearing an intersection, Katie noticed a long line of people waiting to get inside a store. "What's that place?" she asked.

"Ah, Berthillon,"[20] André smiled. "Have you never heard of it?"

Both Katie and Zack shook their heads.

He looked surprised. "It is one of the most famous *magasins*

20 Pronounced Behr-tee-yohn

de glaces[21]—ice cream stores." He turned toward the shop. "You must try it."

"No argument here," Zack said.

Katie, Zack, and Butterball waited across the street while André stood in line. Katie took the opportunity to scan the crowd for an American couple with a little girl, but found no family matching that description.

Soon André appeared with three cones of various flavors. Katie reached for the chocolate, so Zack chose the wild strawberry, leaving the mandarin orange for André.

"Yum," Katie said, licking frantically as the ice cream ran down the cone and across her fingers in the hot summer air. "This is sweet!" Unfortunately, her next determined swipe sent the remaining scoop flying to the ground. Butterball pounced on it like a cat on a mouse.

"Our own vacuum cleaner," Zack said.

After downing the ice cream in one huge bite, the puppy looked up at Katie and wagged furiously, her entire body wiggling. Katie chuckled. "I think Butterball is the *biggest* fan of Berthillon's."

The group soon rounded a corner and headed toward a wide stone bridge spanning a gently flowing river. "This is the Pont Saint-Louis," André said. "In French, *pont*[22] means 'bridge'."

Katie inhaled as her gaze fell just beyond the bridge to an enormous, ornate cathedral, its elaborate pinnacles reaching up to pierce the clouds. André smiled. "The Cathédrale Notre

---

21 Pronounced mag-ah-zahn deh glahs

22 Said through your nose with a nasal sound, pronounced pohn

Dame[23] on the Île de la Cité," he said in an almost reverential tone.

"Notre Dame Cathedral!" Zack looked incredulous. "I've read about it in history books...but I'm actually *seeing* the real Notre Dame!"

Katie looked at André. "Isn't that where the hunchback lives?"

The teenager chuckled. "*Oui*, but only in the book." He gave her a smile.

She felt the heat rush to her cheeks. "Yeah, of course," she nodded, looking away quickly.

"We will go there tomorrow," André said, "but today we will check out the Seine River." He turned to his left and led them down some steep concrete steps just before the bridge. "I will show you on a map sometime how the Seine curves through the center of Paris and divides it almost down the middle," he said over his shoulder.

Katie carried Butterball until they reached the wide stone walkway that ran alongside the river. Setting the puppy down, she felt an instant sense of calm beside the slow-moving water. It seemed so peaceful in the middle of this bustling city.

As they strolled along, Katie kept a firm hold on Butterball's leash so the puppy wouldn't accidentally slip down the steep, fifteen-foot embankment. She was especially glad she was minding the leash when they drew near a couple lounging on a colorful blanket, because Butterball made an unexpected lunge for their

23 Pronounced Cah-tey-drawl No-trah Dahm

bread and cheese picnic. Fortunately, Katie was able to pull the puppy up short just in time.

Soon they passed a group of chattering girls who immediately turned to *ooh* and *aah* at the adorable animal. Katie took Butterball over when they asked to pat her, and the puppy ate up the attention like a pint-sized movie star. Finally Katie pulled Butterball away and continued on past lots of people soaking in the warm afternoon sun—but no couple with a blonde girl. She felt frustration building inside her. *I want that little girl to get her special puppy back!*

When they came to an unoccupied spot by the edge of the river, Katie sighed. "André," she called, "could we stop for a while?"

"*Bien sûr*,"[24] he said. "Of course." He went over and sat down on the edge, letting his legs hang over the steep embankment like he must have done a hundred times before.

Katie slid the puppy's leash from her wrist and held it lightly as she started to sit on the ledge beside him. Glancing over at André, she smiled, feeling self-conscious and awkward as she swung her legs around and struggled to keep her balance.

In the next instant, she was sliding down the embankment, piercing the air with a long shriek, followed by a *splash!*

The cool, murky river momentarily closed over her head. Katie quickly clawed her way back up to the surface. Spitting out some water, she looked up at André and Zack who were on their feet, staring at her with open mouths. André called down

---

24 Pronounced bee-ehn soor

anxiously, "*Vous allez bien?*...I mean, are you okay?"

Katie swiped at a strand of algae hanging over her eyes and began treading water. "I'm all right," she said, scraping something else slimy off her cheek. Then she noticed the crowd staring down at her. *I just wish I could disappear right now!* she wanted to add. To top it off, she could tell Zack was trying not to laugh as he held Butterball. *When I get up there I'm going to push* ***him*** *in,* she thought, flipping some strands of hair from her face.

André was motioning toward the bank a little downstream. "Swim to the steps," he was saying.

Katie spied the narrow cuts in the steep embankment nearby and paddled over to them. In a horribly ungraceful way, she managed to get one of her feet onto the slippery bottom step. Then she crawled hand-over-hand back up to the walkway.

When she reached the top, a small cheer rose from the crowd. Katie smiled weakly, but kept her head down as André guided her through the curious throng and back toward the bakery. As they walked, Katie could see a wet trail following her, marking her entire route home.

Zack trotted up beside her. "Are you okay?"

"Don't talk to me," she muttered, not turning her head.

"Huh? What'd I do?"

Katie refused to talk further as she slogged on. Finally they slipped back through the passageway and climbed up the several flights of spiral stairs. When they reached the top landing, André said, "Wait here," and he disappeared down the hall.

Katie closed her eyes, but could hear pings of water hitting the hardwood floor beneath her. Without looking, she knew

Zack had moved around in front of her. "Hey, I think Butterball wanted to go for a swim with you," she heard him say. Katie knew that voice. Without even opening her eyes she could see the grin on his face.

"It's not funny," she mumbled, looking up and giving him her best glare.

Zack turned his head away, stifling a laugh. "Actually, it *was* pretty funny," he said quietly.

"It was *humiliating!*"

"Here you go," said André, reappearing with several thick towels.

His action brought an instant flashback of Stubby appearing with a pile of threadbare towels while she and Zack stood there dripping from the Bahamian thunderstorm. But this time it was only her…and it hadn't been a rainstorm.

As Katie tried to dry off, she glanced up at André. "Butterball must have knocked me off balance," she said, looking back down quickly so she wouldn't have to meet his eyes. She could, however, feel Zack staring at her.

"I am glad you are okay," André said kindly. "I will be down in the bakery, *oui?* You can just clean up and rest. We will not go out anymore today."

I'll bet you don't ever want to be seen with me again, Katie thought as she trudged down the hall.

After gathering some dry clothes, Katie locked the bathroom door and stewed while she took a long shower. The only positive thing that happened was discovering the small shower stall to be just the right size for a good wash.

As she pulled on her clean clothes, Katie's mind began replaying the entire river episode again. And there was Zack standing on the bank—grinning. *He loves to make fun of me,* she thought, clenching her teeth. *He makes me so mad!*

All at once an image of the pastor on Elbow Cay popped into her mind. She could hear him talking about Joseph, and about how he had forgiven his mean brothers for selling him into slavery. Then she remembered the preacher talking about Jesus and about how He had forgiven those who crucified Him.

Staring at her reflection in the bathroom mirror, Katie let out a long sigh. *I learned that I'm supposed to forgive like Jesus forgave...but that's sure not easy.* "Bummer," she mumbled. "I *knew* I was going to have to practice that again."

Katie looked down at the sink. *I guess it's not really worth staying mad about,* she decided. *And...I probably* ***did*** *look pretty funny.* The corners of her mouth started to turn up ever so slightly as she began combing out her hair.

After ringing out her "river clothes" as best she could, Katie hung them from the large towel rack in the bathroom. When she got back to Émilie's room, she found Zack sitting on her bed, watching Butterball sleep in her large cardboard box stuffed with towels. The puppy looked utterly content.

"Hey," Zack said, looking up.

"Hey back," she gave him a slight smile.

"You okay?"

"Yeah, I'm fine." Her smile began to grow. "That was *crazy!*"

Zack grinned, obviously relieved that she wasn't still mad.

"Yeah, you looked pretty funny with that seaweed hanging off your head."

Katie swung her arms wide. "Well, I've made my grand entrance into Paris!" They both burst out laughing.

After a moment, Zack grew more serious again. "But Katie, how come you told André that Butterball knocked you into the river?"

Katie looked surprised and hesitated for a second, then shrugged. "It's not a big deal."

Zack shook his head. "But…it wasn't true."

Katie frowned. "Who made you my boss?"

Looking down at the floor, Zack didn't respond for a minute. Then he said softly, "I'm not trying to boss you around. It just made me think of something my dad is always quoting from some ol' preacher guy named Finney. He says 'a person who's dishonest in little things isn't really honest in anything.'"

The only sound in the room came from a sputtering motorbike below the open window. Finally Katie said, "Just forget it, okay?" She turned away…but Zack's words still stung.

Right then a noisy yawn followed by a yelp came from the corner as Butterball woke up and demanded some attention. "Come here, girl," Katie said, going over and scooping the round puppy into her arms, relieved for a way to change the subject.

Zack remained quiet for a few awkward moments, then said, "Wanna take her out to the courtyard?"

Katie hesitated. "Well…sure."

Playing tug-o-war with Butterball and an old rag brought things back to normal. Soon André joined them, setting down some dog food for the puppy. "No more pizza rolls for you," Katie announced with a smile.

Butterball was fed and placed back in her box as the family gathered around the table for dinner. Monsieur Boulanger gave a short prayer in French, then began passing platters of food. From the conversation that followed, it didn't appear that André had mentioned the river incident to his parents, for which Katie was incredibly grateful.

After supper, Zack and Katie both headed straight to their rooms, since it had actually been their bedtime when they first arrived in Paris. It had been a long day.

Just before climbing into bed, Katie propped open her window to try and cool the muggy summer air. Then she bent down and ran a gentle hand over the puppy's silky fur. "Good night, Butterball," she said softly.

A warm tongue wrapped around her fingers.

Katie smiled and knelt down by the box. "Please Lord," she began, closing her eyes, "please help us find Butterball's family. I don't want her to go to the dog pound. And please help me learn whatever I'm supposed to learn here. Amen."

As Katie snuggled into Émilie's silky sheets, her mind began to replay Zack's voice: *A person who's dishonest in little things isn't really honest in anything.* Katie squeezed her eyes tight. *I don't want to think about that. Besides, it really wasn't a big deal.*

Katie tried hard to focus on André, Notre Dame, and all the stylish people sipping coffee at the sidewalk cafés, and soon she drifted off to sleep—until her heart just about hit the ceiling when a piercing wail shattered the air!

CHAPTER 4

That same Monday evening, a family of three was dining in a fancy hotel restaurant three blocks north of Notre Dame. Glancing out the window beside their table, Veronica Stewart sat lost in thought, looking down at the bustling street illuminated by city lights. *So much has happened….* She twirled a strand of her dark blonde hair around an index finger for several minutes, then turned and began helping her young daughter cut a roll. "Lucy, how about some butter, sweetie," she said, opening a small packet.

The girl silently knifed some of the soft yellow spread onto her bread. Then her hand froze. Looking up at her mother with pleading eyes, Lucy said in a small voice, "Why can't we go search again tomorrow?"

Mrs. Stewart saw her husband run a hand through his jet

black hair. Meeting his daughter's eyes, he gave her a forced smile.

Reaching over, Mrs. Stewart smoothed her daughter's blonde ponytail. "Honey, we've been through this many times," she said gently, looking at the girl with sympathetic blue eyes. "We've walked around the whole area, the police know, the hotels know. If they find your puppy, they will tell us."

"But maybe they won't know she's *my* puppy," the girl protested.

"Lucy," her father said in a kind but firm voice, "we've done everything we can. We need to try and enjoy Paris for the few days we have left here, okay? Can you do that?"

The girl sighed. "I still think we should keep looking for her. She couldn't have gone too far—she's got really short legs."

Mrs. Stewart looked over to meet her husband's dark brown eyes. "Veronica," he said, rising from the table, cell phone in hand, "I need to go make a call."

Reading the frustration in his face, she gave him a slight smile and watched as her husband's lean frame disappeared around the far corner. Then she turned back to Lucy. "Sweetie," she said, putting the rest of the butter on the girl's roll, "I promise you that everywhere we go tomorrow we'll keep an eye out for the dog. And tomorrow morning we're going back over to Notre Dame—" she pointed, "so we can look around there again."

Lucy stared at her plate.

"And," her mother continued, "we've still got until Friday before we drive the SUV—'Big Blue' as you call it—down to

Marseille[25] for Daddy's new job. So we still have some time to find her."

Just then a waiter appeared. "Another café, Mrs. Stewart?"

She lifted her coffee cup. "Yes, please. Oh…I mean, *s'il vous plait*,"[26] she said, smiling at the man standing straight and tall in a formal white waist coat.

"*Très bien,*" he nodded, filling her cup. The waiter then glanced at Lucy's sad face, and back to Veronica Stewart. "You have such a pretty daughter," he said.

Lucy looked up at the man with her teary blue eyes.

"You are nine?" he asked the girl.

"Eight," Lucy said softly.

"*Oui*, my daughter is eight as well." He smiled at her. "Can I get you anything?"

Lucy shook her head.

"Okay. *Merci*,"[27] he said, turning to leave.

As the waiter disappeared, Veronica Stewart brushed her hair back from her face and moved closer to Lucy. "Honey," she said, wrapping an arm around the girl's shoulders and giving her a squeeze, "I know it's been hard, moving away from all your friends in Ohio and coming over here to a foreign country. We thought Grammy's puppy might make it easier…but that didn't quite work out." She hugged the girl again. "When we get to Marseille and your father settles in at the American consulate, we can get you another puppy."

---

25 Pronounced Mahr-say, a city in the south of France

26 Pronounced see voo play, meaning please

27 Pronounced mare-see, meaning thank you

Lucy's head dropped even farther. "I don't want another puppy. I want...Butterball," she choked out, a large tear dropping into the red napkin in her lap.

Mrs. Stewart's heart hurt for her only child. She had *so* wanted this move to go well. "I know, sweetheart," she said, laying her cheek on Lucy's head. "I know."

Mr. Stewart reappeared and sat down. Looking at his daughter he said, "Hey Luce, tomorrow we're going to see some fascinating things. Notre Dame is an *amazing* place, with gorgeous stained-glass windows and all. And we can go up in the towers and look at the funny gargoyles[28] sticking their tongues out. Then we'll go to the top of the Eiffel Tower and see Paris from w-a-y up high. That should cheer you up, sweetie."

Lucy didn't respond, but she did reach for her roll.

Well, her mom thought, *at least she's going to eat something. It's a start.*

Mrs. Stewart met her husband's eyes. "Russell, when do you think we can go to the ancestor registry and search for my relatives?"

He thought for a second. "How about Wednesday morning before we see Versailles?"

She exhaled and subconsciously started twisting the strand of her hair again. "I really hope I can find some information about my grandparents. It's such a good opportunity with you being sent here to France." She turned to gaze absently out the

28 Pronounced gar-goyls, grotesque carved figures in the shapes of humans or animals

window once more, adding softly, "It would be so nice to know some family here."

"I know, Ronni," she heard him say. "I know how much you're going to miss your friends...and your sister." His voice dropped as he added, "You two are so close."

At hearing his words, she closed her eyes. *Close? More like inseparable!* She twirled her hair more forcefully.

After a few silent moments, Veronica Stewart took a breath and turned to her husband again. "I'm happy for you, Russell. Really." She gave him a gentle smile. "This job at the consulate is such a great advancement for you...and I'm sure I'll be fine." Her voice trailed off.

"It certainly would help in finding your relatives if you had more to go on," Mr. Stewart said.

She nodded. "I know, but I just keep running into dead ends."

"Well hey, we're in Paris," her husband said, obviously trying to sound enthusiastic. "And incredible things can happen here, right, Lucy?"

She looked up. "I hope so."

Folding his napkin beside his plate, he indicated it was time to go.

Veronica Stewart caught his eye and shook her head, making a discreet motion that Lucy was eating.

"Oh!" he said. "No hurry." Turning around in his chair, he raised his coffee cup slightly. "Waiter?"

Katie bolted upright in her bed. The high-pitched, distraught cry came from somewhere so close that it caused her heart to pound like a bass drummer on steroids. *What on earth—?*

Again the yowl sliced through the still night—and instantly Katie knew what it was. Leaping out of bed, she rushed over to the corner. City lights from outside illuminated a sad little puppy sitting on her haunches, head pointed straight up, pleading not to be left alone.

Katie picked up the tiny noisemaker. "You sure have big lungs," she said, holding the puppy close. "Did you need some attention?" she cooed as Butterball's tail began to wag.

Just then the door opened a crack and André's voice called through, "Katie? Is everything all right?"

Carrying the puppy over to the door, Katie peeked through the crack. "We're fine," she whispered. "Butterball just didn't like being left alone in the box."

Katie heard Zack's voice in the dark behind André. "Spoiled dog. She'll just have to learn."

André turned away from the door and said softly, "We cannot have her howling all night. She will wake up the entire block!"

Katie came to the rescue. "She can sleep with me, André. That should keep her quiet."

"Okay, *bien*. See you in the morning."

Katie grinned. *This will be great!*

As the boys' footsteps faded down the hall, Katie heard Zack muttering, "That's one spoiled puppy."

Retrieving some towels from Butterball's box, Katie created a little nest on the bed, then laid the puppy beside her. "There you go, girl," she said, stroking the golden fur. "That should make you happy."

Butterball scooted over closer to Katie, stretched her short legs straight out, and soon both of them were fast asleep.

The next morning Katie awoke to find herself crammed up against the wall with the puppy enjoying the remainder of the bed. Katie carefully rolled over and slid Butterball away. "Good morning, bed hog," she said as the puppy's tail began to thump against the sheets.

In her next breath, Katie caught the delicious aroma of warm, fresh-baked bread filling the house. "Yum! What a way to wake up!" she said, giving the puppy a pat.

Butterball yawned, then licked her little black nose.

After quickly pulling on some clothes, Katie took the puppy to the courtyard, fed her, and got her settled back in her box. Finally, Katie was able to get herself ready for the day. Sunlight streamed through the open window as she combed her hair, and from somewhere down the street the music of a golden-voiced soprano almost made Katie hold her breath. "That's incredible!" she said, poking her head out the window to see if she could find the soloist.

When Katie arrived in the dining room, Zack was finishing off a piece of bread slathered with jelly. Purple stains ran up from both sides of his mouth.

"Good?" Katie said, pointing at his face to indicate the mess.

With bulging cheeks, the boy could only nod and smile slightly.

Katie shook her head as she took a seat. She guessed that Monsieur and Madame Boulanger had been downstairs since the wee hours of the morning to start baking for the day.

Soon André appeared, dressed in his vest, red neck scarf, and beret. "How did everything go last night, Katie?"

"Great!" she said. "Butterball loved sleeping with me—but that tiny puppy managed to hog the entire bed."

André smiled. "At least she was quiet." He paused. "And are you ready to go to Notre Dame?"

"Absolutely!" Katie said, grabbing the remaining half of her croissant and jumping up. "I'll go get Butterball."

Zack stuffed one more roll into his mouth and followed her out.

With the accordion slung over his back, André led the way up the street. He had tied a matching red scarf around Butterball's neck, so the musician and puppy made an eye-catching pair.

After crossing the Pont Saint-Louis, they turned onto a wide sidewalk that ran between the Seine River on their left and a grassy area alongside Notre Dame on their right. André looked up at the church and said, "Notre Dame marks the very center of Paris, because all distances are measured from the cathedral. And we recently celebrated its 850th birthday."

"That's really old!" Katie said, staring up at the enormous white-stone building. "And it's got so many towers and levels and pointy things. I'll bet someone could get lost in there and never be heard from again."

André chuckled. "It is a big place, Katie. I have heard that it is longer than one of your entire football fields."

"Wow, that's big!" Zack said, craning his neck to look up. "And what are all those funny-looking creatures sticking out from the balconies and rain spouts way up there?"

"Those are the famous gargoyle statues," André said. "They are creatures originally placed there with the idea of warding off evil." He paused for a second, adding, "But of course we know *God* is all-powerful, not some ugly hunk of stone."

Zack nodded. "Definitely."

André decided to set up at the end of the grassy area, just around the corner from the massive church's entrance. Katie watched in fascination as he placed his beret upside down on the ground in front of him, pulled the accordion up to his chest, and secured the straps around his shoulders.

"How about a little French *musette?*" the teenager suggested, beginning a lively waltz that got Katie's foot tapping. Beside her, Butterball seemed equally captivated, cocking her head as André's fingers raced up and down the keyboard.

Katie couldn't take her eyes off the boy and his instrument. "That's amazing!" she exclaimed, smiling from ear to ear. "I've never heard anything like it. It sounds like an entire orchestra in a box!"

André's fingers ran deftly across the keys on the right, while his other hand marked out a fast 3/4 rhythm on the left-hand buttons. In no time, a small crowd had gathered, drawn by the delightful tune. A few coins clinked into the beret.

As soon as André finished the piece, people began to applaud.

Bowing slightly he said, "*Merci, merci,*" then launched into a slower, romantic-sounding piece, followed by another upbeat French number.

Katie stood nearby, mesmerized by the rich sounds of the accordion and the joy of watching people respond—until all at once she remembered why they were there. *I've got to look for Butterball's owners!* She immediately stepped back from the crowd so she could scan for the American family.

After performing for about twenty minutes, André spoke to the crowd in French, then swung the accordion off his back and rested it on the sidewalk. Katie hurried over to him. "That was *incredible!*" she exclaimed. "I've never heard an accordion before. It sounds like a whole symphony coming out of there!"

"Yeah," Zack agreed, "that was great!"

André grinned. "*Merci*. The *accordéon* is very popular in France and all of Europe."

"Is it hard to play?" Katie asked.

"All instruments take time to master," he said. "I still have much to learn. But anyone can play if they are willing to practice." He smiled at her. "I know many girls your age who are studying the *accordéon*."

Katie's eyes lit up. "That would be so awesome! I play the piano really well, so maybe I'd be good."

Zack frowned. "I didn't know you played piano."

Katie ignored him and continued looking at André. "Aren't you going to perform anymore?"

"*Oui, oui*...but I need a short break." He smiled at her. "How about your first lesson now?"

"Right now?" Katie gulped. *I just told him I'm good on the piano….*

Zack was grinning. "Go for it, Katie. Show us those great piano skills."

André sat down on the low curb and motioned for Katie to sit beside him.

Wanting to look good for the teenager, she smiled weakly. "Uh, okay," she said, dropping down beside him. He placed the accordion on her lap and showed her how to put her arms through the straps. It all felt incredibly awkward, and a knot started to grow in the pit of her stomach.

André moved behind her and adjusted the straps to fit her smaller frame, then explained how the keys on the right side of the instrument were just like piano keys. "When you pull on the bellows with your left arm, it allows you to play the keys," he said.

Katie swallowed hard.

"Why don't you start with a simple piece you know on the piano," he said, sitting back to watch.

Even if she had wanted to get up and run, she couldn't have moved. The accordion was too heavy. *What am I going to do?*

Then it hit her. *Maybe I'll get that supernatural ability again, like riding Tango, and roping, and scuba diving!* Katie started to smile. *Hey, this could be really amazing!* Looking up at Zack, she grinned and thought, *Watch this,* as she gave the bellows a mighty heave with her left arm and pressed some keys on the right.

CHAPTER 5

Having experienced miracles at Cassidy Ranch and in the Bahamas, Katie felt pretty confident, and a little cocky too—until some ghastly discordant sounds blared from the instrument. She hurriedly moved her hand and tried pressing different keys, with the same horrible results. *This can't be happening!*

André looked at her with large eyes. "Just pull on the left and play some single notes with your right hand, like you do on the piano," he instructed patiently.

"O...kay," she said sheepishly, trying again. Once more, a random jumble of notes came out.

"Wow, Katie, that's great!" Zack said, clapping. "Should I pass the hat around?"

Katie's face felt as red as the scarf around Butterball's neck. Looking down, she said barely above a whisper, "André, I don't really play the piano very well."

André didn't say anything for a moment, but he seemed to be thinking. Finally he asked, "Do you want me to take the *accordéon* off of you?"

She just nodded, and he stood to help slip the instrument's straps off her shoulders. As he lifted the accordion from her lap and set it down beside him, he said, "Katie, why did you tell me you played piano well?"

"I don't know."

André sat back down and took a breath. Slowly he said, "Do you remember when I told you my father is a decent man with good principles?"

Katie nodded.

"Papa is determined to run his business honestly, and he has made sure that my sister and I know the importance of always telling the truth. In fact, I just read a Bible verse yesterday that said, 'It is better to be poor and godly than rich and dishonest.'"[29]

"I'm sorry," Katie said softly. "I know I shouldn't have told you that. I *have* taken piano lessons…I'm just not very good."

André shifted, looking a little uncomfortable. "No, no, I understand. I know you did not mean anything bad," he said quickly. "I just always believe we are to be completely truthful."

"Okay," Katie said, hoping they were done with this topic.

After an awkward moment, André spoke up. "*Mais bien sûr!*[30] But of course!" His face lit up. "I have something that

29 Proverbs 16:8

30 Pronounced Meh bee-yen soor

helps me each day."

Katie stole a peek at him from the corner of her eye. The teenager looked more excited than she had seen before.

"*Oui.* What a difference it has made in my life," he continued. "Katie, may I show you something when we get back home?" His dark brown eyes seemed to almost sparkle. "I think you will like it very much."

She nodded, curious what it could be. "Sure," she replied, smiling a little.

"*Bien.*" He rose to his feet. Katie met his eyes and didn't see any anger or judgment there. Only kindness.

Zack moved over toward them and gave Katie a funny look, but didn't say anything. She couldn't tell what he was thinking, but didn't have time to dwell on it because André said to them, "I believe I could use your help, if you are willing."

"Okay," they said together.

"When I finish playing, would you take the beret and walk around the crowd saying, '*Vous aimez la musique?*'[31] It means, 'Do you like the music?'"

Zack attempted to repeat the phrase, and André corrected a word. When Zack tried it again, André said, "*Exactement.*"[32]

"That's fun!" Zack said.

Then Katie tried, and André corrected her. She tried again, and received further coaching. After about the fourth attempt, Katie felt her face turning red again, and André looked sympathetic.

31 Pronounced Voo eh-may lah moo-zeek?

32 Pronounced eg-zact-eh-mahn, meaning exactly, or perfect

"Maybe you could carry the beret and Zack could say the phrase," he suggested.

Katie turned frustrated eyes on Zack as he handed her the cap. With a shrug Zack said, "I study languages at home, Katie, so I've had a head start."

She rolled her eyes.

"Or," Zack added, "you could play the accordion while I take the beret." He jumped back quickly so she couldn't smack him.

This isn't my day, Katie thought, bending down to tie Butterball's leash to a low trellis beside André.

As the accordion music started again and another crowd gathered, Katie could hear Zack nearby, quietly practicing his phrase. After two numbers, André stopped and thanked everyone for their applause, then nodded toward Zack and Katie. Zack dove into the crowd, repeating, "*Vous aimez la musique? Vous aimez la musique?*" while Katie followed, holding out the beret with a somewhat forced smile.

After about half an hour, André lowered his accordion to take another break. Zack excitedly counted the coins while Katie quietly stroked Butterball.

"Katie," she heard André call, "would you and Zack like to go inside Notre Dame before lunch while I watch for the American family out here? I will keep an eye on the puppy."

"Yeah!" Zack said from beside her. He punched Katie's arm lightly. "Come on, Katie."

She nodded. "Okay." *That sounds way more fun than following along behind Zack with a hat.* Stealing a look at André, Katie found him smiling at her, and she couldn't help the shy smile that formed on her own face.

Zack took off toward the front of the enormous cathedral, making Katie trot to keep up with him. Stopping just outside to look up at the statues around the three arched doorways, Zack said, "Hey, Katie, look at that guy." He pointed toward a headless figure. "He's standing there holding his own head in his hands."

Katie stared up at the statue. The stone figure, along with Zack's endless enthusiasm, forced her to chuckle. "Well, at least he didn't *lose* his head," she quipped.

Zack grinned. "Let's go inside."

They followed the crowd through one of the arched doorways and found themselves in a long, massive hall. Rows of seats ran all the way to the front, flanked by marble pillars supporting a balcony all the way around. Blue stained-glass windows beamed soft light into the great room. Far ahead, just beyond a simple altar, stood a marble statue of Mary with the crucified Jesus across her lap, reminding everyone of His sacrifice for their sins. A large golden cross rose up behind. "Wow," was all Katie could say.

Zack's voice gave her a start when he whispered from behind her, "Let's walk around."

Joining the flow of tourists, they strolled around the sanctuary, observing racks of prayer candles, various marble statues, and enormous rose windows. Zack stopped to study a long row of wood carvings depicting Christ's appearances after He had risen from the grave.

"Look!" Katie whispered, tugging on Zack's sleeve and

pointing toward a poster. "There's a gigantic bell in the south tower, and we can go up and see it."

"But it says it costs money to go up there," Zack showed her.

Katie produced some coins from her pocket. "Mr. Gateman gave us some spending money, remember?" She held them out toward Zack. "André called them Euros.[33] Let's go see how much it costs."

Back outside, they found a line snaking along beside the cathedral toward an entrance to the towers. A bored-looking guard sat by the gate. Katie got his attention, showed him the coins, pointed to herself and Zack, then pointed at the tower. The guard looked over the money, shook his head, pointed back at the coins, and raised one finger.

"You've only brought enough for one of us, Katie," Zack said. He paused, then smiled at her. "That's okay. You go. I think I should get back and help André with the beret thing anyway."

Katie hesitated. She *really* wanted to climb the tower and see the bell, as well as view Paris from above. *But I should be looking for the puppy's owners.*

Zack must have read her mind, because he quickly said, "I'll be sure to keep an eye out for Butterball's family, okay?"

"Um…okay," she said. "You're sure?"

"Yeah, it's fun to speak French and go through the crowd," Zack nodded.

He looked like he meant it, and Katie *wasn't* excited about

33 Pronounced Yur-ohs. The Euro is the currency for a confederation of countries throughout Europe.

trailing behind him with the hat, so she told him she'd be back in no time.

The line moved rapidly, until Katie was about to hand the man her money. Just then, another guard appeared and spoke to the coin collector. After their brief conversation, the guard put his hand out to stop Katie from going with the group and started to pull a chain across the entrance.

"What's wrong?" she asked.

"Repairs," he said with a very strong French accent. "No more people today."

"Oh, please…" she gave him her best pleading face. "I'm just one little girl."

He hesitated, looked her over, then nodded slightly and pulled the chain back to let her through.

"Thanks so much!" she called, bounding after the group.

Up she went, following the others around the corkscrew marble steps. On and on they climbed, until Katie groaned, "Over 400 steps. My poor legs!"

About the time she considered stopping for a rest, they reached two short, narrow doors opening into a room. Inside hung a *gigantic* bell from thick rafters. Immediately Katie pictured a pathetic hunchback swinging from a rope below it. Then she whistled softly when she read that it used to take sixteen men to ring the bell, since it weighed over 28,000 pounds. Fortunately the ringing was now mechanized.

Katie smiled when she read further that the bell had been baptized and given a name. "That must have been one big bath-tub!" she said softly to herself.

A lady tour guide standing near her replied, "I think they probably just sprinkled it with water."

"Oh!" Katie giggled at being overheard.

After the bell tower, the group continued up a few more winding stairs until they reached the top of the south tower. As they circled high above the plaza, Katie gazed down at the people far below, appearing like tiny ants running here and there. Looking back over the city, she breathed in deeply and grinned. *Paris—it's simply amazing!*

Beside her a voice said, "And there's the Eiffel Tower." It was the same tour guide who had spoken to her by the bell.

"Oh my gosh!" Katie said, studying the intricate steel structure off in the distance. "I'm seeing the Eiffel Tower!"

After a moment, Katie pointed to one of Notre Dame's tall grey spires close by. "Those statues along the tower, who are they?"

"Those are the twelve apostles," the woman said. Then she waved her hand toward the balconies below them. "They are *much* nicer than all those gargoyles."

Katie wrinkled her nose as she peered at the grotesquely shaped creatures resembling monkeys, lions, eagles, and various flying creatures. "Those are...freaky."

Right then a guard by the stairwell called out that it was time to go back down. Katie lingered a minute longer for one final bird's-eye view of the city. "It really is beautiful," she sighed, then hurried to catch up as the last person disappeared down the staircase.

As she descended, Katie found herself lost in thought. *It*

doesn't matter that I can't speak French or play the accordion. It's just so incredible to be here in this magical city! Of course we've ***got*** *to get Butterball back to that little girl. I think that must be my important job.*

Just as she was starting to think maybe she should hurry and catch up to the group, a red door beside the stairwell caught her attention. Curious, she went over to it and pulled on the small knob handle—and the thick wooden door swung open. "Yes!" Katie said, taking a few steps onto the deserted balcony.

Thunk! The heavy door swung shut behind her. Katie whirled around and tried the handle, but it didn't turn. She pulled on the door…nothing. She tried pushing…it didn't budge an inch. Spying a tiny window high in the door, she stood on tiptoes and yelled, "Help! I'm trapped! Help me!" She banged on the door with her fists, then stopped to listen. Not a sound came from the other side.

Turning around, Katie abruptly jumped backward. Perched right beside her on the balcony ledge sat a ghastly gargoyle statue eating a large stone chicken. Up close, the creature was about the same size as her, and in the late morning shadows, it almost looked real.

She hurried past the frightening figure and walked a short distance on the narrow balcony to see if she could raise attention. A waist-high stone wall with more gargoyles ran along one side, with the wall of the building on the other. It quickly became apparent that this part of the tower and its balconies were set far back from the pedestrian areas below. *No one will* ***ever*** *see or hear me here,* she thought, her heart beginning to sink. *Plus, there are* *no more groups coming up here today, and Zack and André will have no idea where I am!*

As she looked back toward the door and the evil creature beside it, Katie felt an enormous lump growing in her throat. *They're going to find my bones a hundred years from now.* Sliding her back down the wall and hugging her knees to her chest, she uttered in a small plaintive voice, "Somebody help me!"

Chapter 6

Katie sat curled up for what felt like forever. Every time she looked up, she was sure the gargoyles had inched closer, laughing and sticking their tongues out at her. *They're like vultures circling over a dying animal.* Even though the midday sun crept into the narrow space where she huddled, a shudder ran through her.

Dropping her head against her knees, Katie said quietly, "Lord, I know I haven't been totally honest about some things lately, like telling Mom I wasn't reading under the covers, or accusing Butterball of knocking me in the river, or saying I played the piano well. Okay, I haven't been honest about *lots* of things…and I'm really sorry, God. But I sure do need Your help right now. Please send someone to find me…please. And I'll try to do better."

She rose slowly to her feet and glanced over the balcony. *No point in shouting down there,* she thought, turning back toward the door. Concentrating on her feet so she wouldn't have to look at the chicken-eating creature, she reached the heavy door, stood on tiptoes, and grabbed the bars across the tiny window again. "Help!" she started yelling. "Is anyone there? I'm stuck out here! Please help me!"

After calling out a few more times, Katie let go of the bars, dropped back to her feet, and rested her head against the door. *What am I going to do?*

"*Ya quelqu'un?*"[34] came a muffled, deep voice.

Nearly sobbing with relief, Katie stretched as high as she could, latched onto the bars, and started shouting, "I'm out here! Help! I'm stuck! Please help me!"

A moment later, a burly, unshaven face appeared in the small window. "*Que faites vous là?*"[35] he said, obviously surprised to find someone out there.

Katie tried the door handle again, but it didn't budge. Then the door rattled as the man pulled and pushed from the other side. It still didn't open. He muttered something in French, which she guessed meant the same thing she was feeling—*why won't this dumb door open?!*

The small knob began wiggling violently, then came huffing noises—and in the next instant the door flew inward, almost knocking the man down the stairs. As he caught the iron railing

---

34 Pronounced Ya kehl-kuhn, meaning Is anyone there?

35 Pronounced Kehr fett voo lah, meaning What are you doing there?

and regained his footing, Katie rushed through the doorway yelling, "Yay!"

She looked at the hefty man wearing a soiled blue shirt and jeans stained with paint and grease. But to Katie, he was the most handsome person she had seen all day. Without thinking, she threw her arms around his thick neck and said, "Thank you! Thank you!"

He patted her arm and chuckled, then said something that must have been, "Let's go," as he pointed down the stairs.

"Ya hoo!" Katie hollered, rushing down the winding staircase as fast as her legs could carry her. When she reached the bottom, she burst through the door and into the early afternoon sunlight, bolting through a turnstile to freedom. Dashing past the front of the cathedral and weaving through the crowd, she swerved around a tall man holding the hand of a little girl.

Flying around the corner of the church, Katie found André and Zack sitting on the short curb. When they saw her, they immediately jumped to their feet.

"Where have you been?" Zack asked, his mouth set in a line. "You've been gone almost three hours!"

As Katie breathlessly shared her adventure, both boys' eyes grew wider and wider.

"*Incroyable!*" André said. "I am so relieved you are okay."

"Me too!" Katie smiled. "I was afraid all they would find of me was a skeleton!"

Zack grinned. "Or maybe you'd have turned into a gargoyle."

Katie made a face at him.

"It wouldn't take much," he mumbled, quickly jumping out of her reach.

"Let us go eat and celebrate Katie's freedom," André said, gathering his accordion.

"Yes!" Katie exclaimed. She bent down to pick up the wiggly puppy, then looked at André and Zack. "I guess you didn't find her family, huh?"

Zack shook his head. "Butterball was a wonderful attraction, and André got lots of coins...but no one claimed her."

Katie held Butterball close against her. The puppy's warmth felt particularly good after Katie's frightening experience. "Well," Katie said, pressing her face against the puppy's, "we'll just keep looking, huh, girl?"

Once again the pink tongue swiped Katie's nose.

André turned to her. "Oh, Katie," he said, reaching behind him, "while you and Zack were in the *cathédrale*, Butterball and I got you something." He produced a beret much like his, but a lighter shade of red.

Katie's entire face lit up. "I *love* it!" she said, placing it jauntily on her head the way André wore his. She gave him an enormous smile. "Thanks so much! I mean, *merci!*"

He smiled back. "*Vous êtes les bienvenus*[36]...you are very welcome."

When they arrived at the Boulangers' for a late lunch, Zack and André devoured several small pizzas fresh from the oven while Katie ate a melt-in-your-mouth quiche. As soon as they

36 Pronounced Vooz ett lay bee-ehn-vehn-oo

had finished, André disappeared into his room and came out carrying several books. He set them on the dining room table next to Katie. "Here is what I wanted to show you," he said, sitting down and placing a small booklet in front of Katie. He also slid an identical one across the table to Zack.

Katie scooted a little closer.

André met her eyes and said, "Katie, when we receive Christ's forgiveness, the Bible says we are given a new nature inside us."

Frowning slightly, Katie asked, "Like some strange creature living in us?"

André smiled. "No…not like something physical living inside," he said. "But when a person becomes a Christian, God gives him or her a new nature, like a new kind of heart. Then that person wants to do and say things more like Jesus."

Katie grimaced as she immediately thought about all her recent lies.

André continued. "Have you noticed any changes, Katie, since receiving Jesus?"

She bobbed her head. "I haven't wanted to get into fights with my brother Mark—that's a *big* change—and I've felt more loving toward my family."

"Yes, that is your new spiritual nature from God," André nodded. "And I have learned how important it is for us to feed that new nature so it will grow stronger." He paused for a moment, then said, "Think of it like this: when Butterball was born, she received everything inside her to become a full-grown dog. But in order to grow big and strong she needs to eat good food, *oui?* Otherwise, she will be a sick little dog."

Katie nodded, so André continued. "When we receive Christ, we instantly get His nature inside us…but now we need to feed that nature so we will grow into becoming more like Jesus." He looked at her. "Do you understand?"

She scrunched up her face in thought. "But how do we feed the new nature?"

"Well, Butterball wants to eat dog food because that is what her dog nature wants. In the same way, a Christian should feed on the Word of God every day because it is our most important source of spiritual food."

Zack burst in, "I've been learning the same thing at home. Mom keeps saying, 'Whatever you feed, grows.'"

"*Oui*, that is right," André looked at Zack then back to Katie. "If we feed ourselves bad things, like impure programs on TV or the internet, it is like eating garbage, and bad things will come out of our lives. Just like if we fed Butterball junk, she would be sick, and her coat would not shine. But when we feed our new nature the truths of the Bible, then God works through His Word and changes us to be more and more like Jesus."

Katie's eyes started to brighten. "So for my new nature to become stronger and more like Jesus, I have to feed it God's Word. Like Butterball needing to eat good food."

André smiled and said, "*Exactement!*" He reached over and opened one of the books. "This is what I use each morning. It is called *Trente Jours avec Dieu*,[37] which means *30 Days with God*."

37 Pronounced Trahnt Zhur ah-vek Dyuh

He smiled broadly, adding, "This has made *such* a difference in my life."

"How?" Katie asked.

"Well…for example, yesterday morning, before I met you, I played my *accordéon* for a famous teacher. I wanted to make him think I had performed more places than I really have. But I had just read a verse about having a clear conscience before God, so I knew it was more important to tell the truth than to try and make myself look good. God's Word changed my actions."

Katie thought again about her own words lately. *Wow, I really need to feed my new nature!*

"André!" a stern voice called right then from the stairwell below, interrupting their conversation. It sounded like Monsieur Boulanger.

The teenager quickly stood up. "I need to run downstairs. We will talk more later," he said, hurrying toward the steps.

"I'll go too," Zack said, leaping up. He looked at Katie and mouthed, "Dessert."

Katie sat quietly for a few moments, replaying as much of their conversation as she could remember. The idea of feeding her new spiritual nature with God's Word seemed to make sense, and it was obviously very important…but it was all so new. She flipped through the little daily Bible book, but since it was in French, she quickly closed it and headed downstairs to drag Zack away from the sweets so they could play out back with Butterball.

After a game of tug-o-war with the puppy, Katie began

looking anxiously at the back door. *If André doesn't take us to the Eiffel Tower soon, we're going to miss Butterball's family.* She started biting on a fingernail.

Finally André appeared. "*Désolé*[38]—I am sorry," he said. "My father wanted me to work at the bakery today, so I needed to explain how important it is that we find the little girl." His mouth seemed rather tight.

It doesn't look like the conversation went too well, Katie thought, but her sole focus at the moment was to keep Butterball from going to the refuge. "André," she said, "can't you ask your friends or coworkers at the bakery if they might want the puppy?"

"I can ask," the teenager said, "but we must keep looking for her family."

"Yeah," Zack nodded, "it sounds like Butterball is super special to that little girl."

"I know," Katie said softly. *But I also don't want Butterball to end up going to the pound!*

Adjusting the accordion on his back, André replied, "We will look for the family at the Eiffel Tower. Hopefully we can find them."

He led the group toward a nearby metro station, and as they descended into the tunnel, Katie was instantly overwhelmed by the underground maze. Various color-coded passageways with strange names jutted off in every direction. And when André tried to explain a map of the metro system, Katie thought, *It just looks like a giant plate of colored spaghetti.*

---

38 Pronounced dey-zoh-lay

After buying their tickets, André showed them how to poke the slips of paper into a machine that opened the turnstile, then he directed them to the correct tunnel. As Katie followed close on his heels, she kept thinking, *This is another place where I could disappear and never be heard from again!*

While waiting for the train on the wide platform next to the tracks, Butterball sat down and pressed her body up against Katie's leg. "You okay, girl?" Katie said, looking down.

Butterball raised her head and met Katie's eyes, but only gave a small wag.

Katie bent down to pat her. "It's okay," Katie soothed the worried animal. "We've got André here to lead us through this maze."

Butterball pushed her wet nose into Katie's hand.

Soon the train sped into the station and slid to a stop. Its double doors flew open, and several people hurried off. Then André and Zack pushed forward with the crowd to board. Katie, however, decided to wait a moment so that she and Butterball wouldn't get trampled.

When it looked safe enough, Katie took a step into the car, until she felt a tug on the leash about her wrist. Whirling around, she saw Butterball sitting at the end of the rope, refusing to move.

"Come on, girl," Katie urged the frightened puppy, pulling gently on the line. Just as she did, a loud buzzer sounded and the car doors immediately snapped shut on the leash—trapping Butterball on the other side!

Chapter 7

"Butterball got locked out! Help me!" Katie yelled, terrified of the train taking off and Butterball being dragged alongside by her collar.

Right then the metro started to move ever so slightly. "It's going to choke her!" she screamed, pushing her arm against the door to try and ease pressure on the leash.

Practically sailing over the top of several people, André lunged for a large red lever by the door—and the train jerked to a standstill.

"She's still caught," Katie cried out, not knowing how to open the doors.

Someone near her reached over and heaved on one side of the door, sliding it open. In a single leap, Katie scooped the puppy into her arms. As she checked Butterball's neck to make sure the puppy was breathing okay, she heard André calling, "Get back in."

Katie carried the puppy into the car and sat down on one of the small metro seats beside Zack. As she cradled Butterball in her lap, relief swept over her like a wave, and tears began rolling down her cheeks before she could stop them. Droplets landed on Butterball, making little indents in her fur. From the corner of Katie's eye, she could see Zack looking at her, so she turned her face toward the window.

"It's okay, Katie," Zack said softly. "Butterball's fine."

Katie nodded without turning her head—but she was *very* glad her best friend was there.

Soon a conductor appeared, and once André had explained the situation, the train started to move again. As the car sped along, making stops at various metro stations, Katie was grateful for the time to compose herself. Zack didn't say anything else, but periodically he would reach over and pat Butterball, or tousle the puppy's head a little. Butterball seemed utterly content lounging across Katie's lap, her head draped over the girl's arm.

Finally Katie glanced at Zack and said, "To look at her, you'd never know she just about got strangled."

"I don't think she knows it," Zack smiled, "so we won't tell her."

Katie gave him a tenuous smile and let out a long breath.

While the car jostled on, Katie's thoughts turned to Mr. Gateman's note. *I'm pretty sure my job here is to find Butterball's owners—and I'm so glad she's okay!* Then she frowned slightly. *But I don't get the part about my relationship with my dad and about how I'm going to be changed.* Katie couldn't dwell further on the puzzling note, however, because just then the car pulled into their station.

Ascending out of the metro into the humid summer air, Katie took a deep breath, glad to be back above ground. As she did, her eyes landed on a long expanse of manicured lawn just ahead. Enormous trees formed a border on both sides, marking a grand pathway straight toward the golden Eiffel Tower. Seeing all the couples around the monument relaxing on blankets or walking hand in hand made Katie sigh. "It's *perfect.*"

Beside her, André spoke with obvious pride. "*Oui*, it is our most famous attraction." He gazed up at the structure, and Katie could see the admiration in his eyes.

"Where'd it get its strange name?" Zack asked.

André smiled and looked at the boy. "The Eiffel Tower is named for the man who designed it in 1899, Gustave Eiffel."

"Wow," Zack said, "I didn't know it was that old!"

"It was built for a World's Fair, to show that France was also a world power," André replied. "This was the tallest building in the world, until your Empire State Building went up."

Katie peered up at the tip top and said, "I wouldn't want to get caught up there in a tornado."

André shook his head. "We do not have tornados here, Katie, but the Eiffel Tower is designed so well that the top sways very little, even in the strongest winds. And up there, on a clear day, they say you can see eighty kilometers…about fifty miles."

Leading them along the grass toward the tower, André said over his shoulder, "We will set up closer where there are more tourists. Hopefully we will find Butterball's family."

I sure hope so! Katie thought, gazing down at the puppy trotting happily beside her. *I'm so glad you're okay, Butterball. You just can't go to the pound!* She shuddered a little, picturing this sweet creature looking out from a cage, awaiting its fate.

Soon, strains of lively accordion music filled the air as André's fingers danced across the keyboard. People immediately began to gather, especially enjoying the sight of Butterball sitting just to André's right, watching his every move. A chuckle would ripple through the crowd every time the puppy cocked her head at a high note.

Katie adjusted her beret to match André's and thought, *I really wish I'd been able to play like that. Accordion music is just so happy!*

Right then, André launched into an entirely different type of music, playing in a way Katie had never heard before. The melody transformed into something rather free-flowing, then eventually returned to the theme and ended with a flourish. When he finished, those gathered around and sitting nearby burst into spontaneous applause.

"What was that?" Katie asked, her mouth gaping.

André grinned. "That was *Take Ten*, a jazz piece by your own Frank Marocco." He acted like she would recognize the name.

Katic shrugged.

"You do not know this name?" André said, looking surprised. "Frank Marocco was from your country—a legend on jazz *accordéon!*"

"Oh," Katie said. "Well...I sure like his music!"

André nodded. "I want to play like him," the boy said, starting another jazz piece.

As people stopped to listen or to set up their picnics nearby, Katie and Zack watched for a family matching the description they needed. Several times Katie's heart leaped at seeing two adults and a blonde child, but when she walked Butterball near them, there was no reaction to indicate they had lost a puppy.

When André eventually stopped for a break, Katie and Zack came over and sat by him while Butterball flopped to her side on the lush grass. André reached down into his beret and pulled out some coins, then looked at the two. "Would you like to go up the Eiffel Tower?"

"Yes!" they both exclaimed, jumping to their feet. "But we have some spending money," Katie said, producing a few bills from her shorts pocket.

"*Bien*," André said, looking at the Euros. Then a twinkle came to his eye. "You have enough for the lift up and a snack… or you can take the stairs if you want to."

"Great!" Zack said. "See ya later, André!" He bounded away.

"Don't forget to look for Butterball's family!" Katie called back as she hurried after the redhead.

André nodded and waved, rising to begin another set of music.

Zack and Katie raced to the paved area under the tower, only to find enormous lines in several directions. Katie edged into one fairly short line, trying to figure out what the sign ahead said. As the crowd began to move, she tapped the shoulder of a teenage girl right in front of her. "Excuse me," she said, "what is this line for?"

"Tickets for the stairs," the girl answered.

Just then a deep voice behind Katie said, "Yeah, but the line starts back *there.*"

Katie whirled around to see a man scowling down at her as he pointed behind him.

"But I was already—" Katie started to argue, when she was forcibly jerked out of the line by her arm.

Stumbling sideways a few steps, she yanked her arm loose. "What are you doing?" she growled at Zack.

"You cut in line. You weren't already there," he said, his eyebrows drawing down.

Embarrassed, she began to defend herself, but Zack had already turned away and was walking toward the end of the line. As she slowly followed, her mind churned. *I **was** standing there. Well...I sorta was...maybe...which I guess is what André just talked to me about.* She shrugged. *Whatever...it's no big deal.*

Katie didn't have long to stew, because the line moved quickly. As soon as they reached the counter and had purchased their tickets, Zack took off like a shot toward the stairs with Katie on his heels.

Up, up, up they wound, racing higher and higher along the metal stairway. As she ran, Katie glimpsed thick steel beams all around them, jutting off in every direction. It was like an oversized LEGO® maze, and she was beginning to feel like an exhausted rat trying to find an exit. "Hey!" she gasped at Zack, who was now several turns above her, "I've already...run up...Notre Dame... today!"

Finally reaching the second viewing level, she found Zack standing there grinning. "Look!" he said, pointing at the last step. "It's numbered. We just ran up 669 steps!"

Katie bent over double. "Feels…more like…six thousand."

"Come on," Zack thumped her on the back. "We gotta buy tickets to go on up to the top."

Panting along behind Zack, she caught sight of the grand view below. Paris sparkled as if it had been doused with a fresh coat of white paint.

Zack found a machine dispensing tickets and imitated the person in front of him to purchase theirs. They crowded onto the next lift going up, and as it began to rise, Katie watched between the tangle of golden steel girders as the people below got smaller and smaller.

When the packed car opened its doors on the top level, Katie and Zack rushed toward the railing. A sea of tourists was already crowded against the wire mesh, cameras aimed at the distant skyline. The two kids squeezed into a small spot, and Zack craned his neck to look down. "Do you think I would hit anyone if I spit from here?"

Katie punched his shoulder. "Look up, you goof." She pointed toward the sky.

"Whoa!" Zack said, raising his head. "Look at that sunset!" He gave a low whistle as he wrapped his fingers around the wire mesh in front of them. Long ribbons of brilliant pinks and oranges streaked across the horizon as lights began twinkling throughout the darkening city below. "Mom would love to see this," he murmured.

Katie smiled, imagining how happy this would make Mrs. Cassidy.

As the sunset slowly faded, the city below burst to life. Riverboats decked in dazzling lights drifted under arched bridges ablaze in white. Tall domed buildings, huge marble monuments, majestic Notre Dame—all glowed against the deepening night sky. Katie shook her head. *Is this real? Can I **really** be in Paris on the top of the Eiffel Tower?*

"This is pretty awesome," Zack said, grinning from ear to ear as he looked out over the gleaming city.

After a few more minutes, they pressed back through the crowd and made their way around the small, high platform. Katie kept an eye out for Butterball's family while Zack stopped to look at various historical displays. In a short time he announced, "I'm starving! Let's go back to the first level. I saw a café there."

"I'm sure you did," Katie smiled. "But we're taking the elevator!"

At the same time Katie and Zack were marveling at the glorious sunset, Lucy and her parents were standing on the level below, also watching the heavenly light show. "That is simply gorgeous," Veronica Stewart sighed. She reached toward Lucy standing in front of her and lovingly pulled back the girl's blonde hair. "Isn't that something, Luce?"

"It's really pretty," she nodded.

Russell Stewart leaned forward and placed a hand on the mesh barrier in front of them. "Reminds me of the amazing sunsets back home right after the clouds—"

Veronica Stewart gave him "the look."

"Yeah..." he cleared his throat, "that *is* an incredible Paris sunset."

Lucy turned to look at her parents. "How 'bout we go look for Butterball now."

Mrs. Stewart smiled. "You don't want to see anything else from up here, honey?"

The girl shook her head. "I just want to find my puppy."

"Okay, Lucy," Mr. Stewart said. "But let's stop at the first level and take a quick look around from there, okay? Then we'll head back to the hotel, in case anyone has reported a missing dog."

After one last, lingering gaze at the blazing horizon, Mrs. Stewart grasped her daughter's hand and followed her husband toward the line for the lift down.

When they reached the first level, Mr. Stewart led the way around the platform, stopping every now and then to read something about the tower's construction, or to point out an important monument to Lucy. Veronica Stewart smiled when she saw Lucy just staring over the railing while her father explained the significance of the Panthéon and the important French citizens buried there.

All at once Lucy gave a cry. "Look, Mom! It's Butterball!" she pointed frantically toward the park below. "See the man with that black box, and the puppy pulling on the leash? I *know* that's Butterball!"

As the girl began hopping up and down, Mrs. Stewart met

her husband's eyes. He shrugged. "It could just be another golden retriever puppy, sweetheart…but let's go and see." He took Lucy's hand.

"I know it's her! I know it!" Lucy insisted as they headed toward the elevator. "We've gotta hurry, Dad!" She pulled on her father's hand as she rushed ahead.

When they reached the line for the car down, Lucy could hardly stand still. "There are so many people! We won't make it on to the first car," she moaned, dancing from one foot to the other.

Mrs. Stewart laid a gentle hand on the girl's shoulder. "We can't run over everybody, sweetie. And the man with the puppy was playing music for the tourists, so they should still be there."

"But it's getting dark," Lucy complained, "and they might go home, and I can't see Butterball from here."

The elevator seemed to creep down toward them. When it opened, a red-headed boy dashed out the doors, followed closely by a girl in a beret. "Everyone's in a hurry," Mr. Stewart said to his wife.

She smiled but didn't reply.

Lucy was right; they didn't fit into the first car, so they had to wait for the next one. When it *finally* arrived, they squeezed in and soon stopped at the ground level.

Lucy practically exploded out the elevator doors, and would have taken off like a bullet if Mr. Stewart hadn't jumped and caught his daughter's hand. "Slow down there, Lucy Lightning. You can't go running off by yourself."

Lucy turned pleading eyes to her father. "Come on, Dad!

We've gotta get to Butterball!"

"Okay, sweetheart, we're going, we're going," he said to his impatient daughter.

They wove their way through the thick evening crowd and reached the edge of the long park, but couldn't see the musician. "They were there," Lucy pointed ahead. "I know I saw them!"

"Let's go look," her father said, trotting beside his daughter, holding tightly to her hand, while Mrs. Stewart followed behind.

They went a ways into the park and looked all around, but there was no musician—and no puppy.

Heartbroken, Lucy collapsed on the ground and burst into tears. Mrs. Stewart knelt beside her and wrapped her arms around the girl, letting her weep. From above, she heard her husband say softly, "I'll go find a cab."

Zack made a beeline from the elevator to the café he'd seen on the first level. Katie started to race after him, but soon realized she was just too tired. By the time she reached the shop, Zack had already ordered. "Come on, Katie!" he called as she dragged in. "What do you wanna eat?"

Katie looked at the selections in a glass case, then saw the prices. "We won't have much money left after this," she commented as she pointed toward a sandwich.

After picking up their orders, Zack decided they should walk around the level while they ate. He would frequently read aloud some description of the panorama before them, but Katie only half listened. *I'm not going to remember all that stuff anyway,* she thought, *and I'd rather just look at Paris.*

Soon they reached the side that overlooked the park where André had been performing. "Those long gardens," Zack was reading, "were originally a parade ground for a Royal Military Academy."

"Uh huh," Katie said, trying to spot André. "Hey, Zack," she said, "I don't see André and Butterball. All I see is a woman and a little girl sitting there."

Zack looked down. "He's probably waiting for us underneath."

"I sure hope so," she said, immediately picturing what it would be like to try and find their way home on the metro alone. "Maybe we'd better go."

"Well…okay," he replied, obviously not quite ready to leave yet. "The stairs are over there."

As they headed toward the steps, Katie looked down at the people below enjoying the pleasant Paris evening. Seeing a white horse hooked to a fancy old-world carriage, complete with driver in black tails and top hat, made her smile. Except…three college-age girls were climbing into the carriage, and one of them was holding a golden puppy—wearing a red scarf around its neck!

CHAPTER 8

"They're taking Butterball!" Katie cried over her shoulder as she sprinted toward the stairwell. Forgetting how tired her legs were, she practically flew down the steps, with Zack close behind.

Reaching the ground, Katie raced toward where she'd seen the horse-drawn carriage and the girls. She soon spied a carriage attached to a gloomy-looking draft horse...but no girls or puppy.

Katie dropped into a fast walk so she wouldn't spook the horse, and hurried up to the driver. He looked as bored as his horse. "Did you see three girls and a puppy?" she blurted out.

The man shook his head and turned away. "No English," he muttered, clearly ending their conversation before it even began.

Katie bit her lip and looked around frantically. *What do we do?*

"Now what?" Zack said from beside her.

Just then Katie heard André's voice calling her name. She turned and saw him running toward them as best he could with the accordion across his back. He was holding up the leash—with Butterball's collar hanging limply at the end. "She wiggled out of it while I was playing my last piece. I went all the way to the end of the park," he motioned breathlessly, "and just got back here."

When Katie explained what she had seen, André rushed over to the carriage driver and began an animated exchange in French. Katie watched impatiently as both men alternately flailed their arms and shook their heads. Finally, André returned and relayed the conversation. "He did see them but doesn't know where they were going. The carriage could take them anywhere—around here, or all the way over to Notre Dame," he said, making a wide sweep with his arm.

"So what do we do?" Katie asked, starting to dig her fingernails into her palms.

André glanced around, then hurried toward a young couple casually leaning against two large mopeds. Another lively discussion occurred, which ended when both riders simultaneously started their motorbikes and waved toward Katie and Zack.

Katie glanced at Zack with eyes that said, *No way!*

André called for them to hurry. "This couple has offered to help you look for the carriage," he explained, helping Katie up behind the young woman. Zack plopped down behind the man.

The woman shouted something in French as she flipped the faceplate of her helmet down with a snap. Katie barely had time to grab the woman's leather jacket before the moped sprang forward with a roar and swerved into the street.

Barreling down the wide avenue, Zack's driver pulled up beside them and yelled something to his girlfriend. Katie looked into Zack's enormous green eyes. *I wonder if my face looks as terrified as his,* she thought, reaching her arms all the way around the woman's waist.

Whatever the two drivers had communicated, it wasn't about safety! They flew up the bricked street, weaving and dodging cars right and left. Katie squealed every time she saw headlights coming straight at them, and each time her driver would dart back into their lane at the last moment possible, missing a collision by mere inches. Car horns blared disapprovingly.

On they roared up the broad boulevard, with Katie's hair flying straight back like a flag in a windstorm. She clamped her teeth tight to stifle a blood-curdling scream. *I'm going to die in Paris!*

Suddenly the traffic came to a stop, but Katie's driver barely slowed down. Instead, she jerked her moped to the right and popped the bike over the curb—and onto a busy sidewalk! Zack's driver followed right behind, and terrified pedestrians began leaping in every direction, popping around like pins in a bowling alley.

Squeezing her eyes shut, Katie opened them just in time to see her driver slam on the brakes, screech sideways, and slide to a stop right beside a tall rack of postcards. *Get me off this thing!* she tried to scream, but the words stuck inside her petrified throat.

As the woman righted the bike, Zack's driver roared up beside them and signaled ahead. At that, both bikes sailed off the curb and back into the heavy evening traffic again.

Just then Katie spied a horse and carriage. Her arm shot out so her driver could see where she pointed. "There!" she shouted over the roar, and the woman nodded.

The motorbike bolted forward like a shot, weaving wildly around cars as they raced toward the buggy. *We found them!* Katie thought with enormous relief. *And I'm still alive!* But when they pulled near the carriage, they saw an older Asian couple on the padded seats, taking in the sights. Katie's heart dropped. She looked over at Zack and shook her head.

The moped drivers flew on past the horse and driver and continued up the boulevard, dodging cars and pedestrians like they were playing a video game. Katie looked past the girl's black helmet and saw a massive monument sitting in the center of the boulevard ahead. The street made a wide circle around the memorial—and there on the opposite side trotted a white horse pulling an open white carriage with three young women inside.

Katie practically pounded on her driver's back, who cut right in front of a black limo and darted over toward the far side. Pulling up closer, Katie could see Butterball nestled in the arms of one of the girls. "That's her!" she yelled.

They slowed down to come alongside the carriage—but Zack's driver roared past them right up to the horse. Startled, the steed bolted forward, breaking into a gallop that sent the passengers flailing. Katie watched in horror as the girls lurched backward—and dropped Butterball!

"No!" Katie screamed as the horse and cart veered into the thick traffic. She could see the girls struggling to grab hold of anything possible…but now there was no sign of her precious puppy. *What if she got thrown out into all these cars!* Katie felt like a nightmare was unfolding right before her eyes.

The motorbikes followed behind until the carriage driver could get his horse back under control and pulled over to the curb. Once everyone had come to a stop, Katie leaped off and ran toward the carriage, passing the buggy driver who had jumped from his perch and was running toward the mopeds, yelling and waving angrily.

When Katie reached the white carriage, she found the girls attempting to sweep the hair out of their eyes and straighten their disheveled clothing. And there, held tightly between one of the girl's feet, sat a trembling Butterball. Katie breathed an enormous sigh of relief and stretched out her arms toward the puppy. In the background she could hear the carriage driver and the bikers yelling at each other.

"Is this your dog?" the girl in the buggy asked, sounding very American.

Katie gave a quick nod as she scooped the frightened animal into her arms. Running a gentle hand over the puppy's head she murmured softly, "Hey girl, it's okay. You're safe. It's all right."

Looking up, Katie said, "My friend was watching the puppy while I went up the Eiffel Tower, and she wiggled out of her collar." Katie hugged Butterball close. "We were afraid we'd lost her."

The girl smiled. "We found her wandering around below

the tower and could tell she was lost, so we thought we'd take her with us to see if we could find her a good home."

Zack spoke from behind Katie. "Do you live here?"

"No," a different girl answered as she tried to run a comb through her tangled locks. "We're from the States. We're just touring Europe during our summer break from college." She looked at her other friends and added, "In fact, I think we're getting out here at the Arc de Triomphe,[39] aren't we, girls?"

As the trio started to climb down, Katie heard one of them say, "That was quite a ride!" Katie wanted to reply, *You thought* ***that*** *was a ride?* but she just smiled, glad to be on solid ground and thrilled to have the puppy safe in her arms.

Zack looked at Katie, put a hand on his red hair, and said, "That was worse than any bucking bronc I've *ever* been on!"

Katie smiled. "Yeah, it was even a billion times worse than being squeezed through the drain of the swimming pool!" They both laughed, mostly out of sheer relief at still being alive.

"So," Zack said, reaching over to pat the horse's haunches, "how do we get back to André?"

"I know one thing," Katie glanced back at the moped drivers who looked like they were ending their heated discussion with the carriage driver, "I'm *not* getting back on that kamikaze scooter!"

"Definitely!" Zack agreed.

Just then the red-faced carriage driver strode over and apologized to the three college girls in halting English. When

39 Pronounced Ark deh Tree-umph. It is a monument honoring those who fought and died for France in the French Revolution and the Napoleonic Wars.

he turned and started toward Katie and Zack, Katie tried to smile sweetly. "I'm sorry the mopeds scared your horse. They scared us too!"

Though it seemed impossible, her comment made the driver's face turn even redder. He waved his arm toward the two young drivers. "Those kids...crazy!"

Katie nodded heartily. "We know—we thought we were going to die!"

He grunted something in French and started to climb back up on his perch behind the horse.

"Uh…" Katie took a few steps toward him, "are you going back to the Eiffel Tower?"

He nodded.

Producing her best pleading look she said, "We don't want to ride those motorbikes again, so…do you think we could go with you?"

The wiry man hesitated, then shrugged and motioned for them to get in.

"Yes!" Zack said, hurrying toward the coach. When he reached the carriage's step, however, he abruptly stopped, bowed at the waist, waved his arm with a flourish, and said, "Your Highness."

Katie giggled and said, "Why, thank you, sir." She stepped into the coach, holding Butterball tightly.

"Oh, and you can come too, Katie," Zack grinned.

"Humph!" she playfully raised her nose at him. As she settled on the black leather seat facing forward, Zack climbed onto the bench across from her. "Well," Katie smiled, "I guess that makes you the Royal Pooper Scooper."

They both laughed, relieved that the terror was over.

The driver clucked to his steed and merged the carriage slowly into the traffic. Katie and Zack called their thanks to the daredevil moped drivers who waved back, cranked up their bikes, and roared away in the opposite direction.

As the big white Percheron trotted slowly around the Arc de Triomphe, Katie sat back against the soft cushion and breathed deeply. *And here we are, with Butterball back in my lap, riding in a white horse-drawn carriage through the streets of Paris. My family would never believe this.*

When they arrived back at the Eiffel Tower, André couldn't have been happier to see them. He even kissed the top of Butterball's nose. And once they finally got back home, all three of them were so exhausted that they practically fell into bed.

Wednesday morning, Katie awoke again to the golden-voiced soprano filling the air with heavenly music from down the street. Still bleary from the events of last night, Katie felt like she was getting dressed in her sleep, and didn't even realize she was pulling on jeans instead of shorts.

After Katie and Zack had eaten, fed Butterball, and taken the puppy outside, André met them in the courtyard and informed them he had to stay and work in the bakery today. Zack looked at the teenager and said, "Well, that's a bummer."

André stared at the rough courtyard stones. "I want very much to go with you," he said softly, "but since I am expected to take over the bakery someday, my father wants me to learn the business."

Katie, noticing his downcast expression, cautiously asked, "Is that what *you* want to do?"

André met her eyes. It was a moment before he said, "No, I very much want to be a musician."

"And play the accordion?" Zack asked.

"Yes, to play professionally. It is not uncommon in Europe. I believe I could do it, and I have received much encouragement from my teacher," he said, turning to gaze across the courtyard. "But there is my father...."

"You've never told him?" Katie said.

André shook his head. "He would not understand."

Silence enveloped them, the only sound being the faint rustling from a small sycamore tree in the center of the yard. After a moment, Butterball, who was nosing at something in the far corner, gave a cute little puppy-sneeze. André went over and picked her up. As he stroked her fur, he looked at Katie with a serious face. "You have two more days to find her owners. I cannot help you today, but I think it is very important that you find them."

Meeting André's eyes, Katie said, "Don't you have any relatives that might want her?"

André paused. "My uncle, Pierre, heard about her and said he might take her...but that is not a good option. He...he is not very kind to animals."

Swallowing hard, Katie persisted. "And what about the workers at your bakery?"

André nodded. "I have asked them. No one wants a large dog."

Starting to feel a bit desperate, Katie said, "How about any of their family or friends?"

Looking down again, André said softly, "One lady told me her sister had to take her big dog to the refuge because she could no longer manage it. When she checked back to see if it had been adopted, it was no longer there."

That sounded like *good* news to Katie, but she noticed André was still staring at the ground. "So someone took the dog?" she asked hopefully.

Without looking up, André just shook his head.

Katie gasped. "So it...." She felt tears starting to form. "I don't know what else to do, André," she said, blinking hard. "I'm praying and everything."

André handed the wiggly animal to Katie. "You must keep searching. And today you must go to Versailles, where the American family is supposed to be."

For a moment no one spoke. Finally Zack asked, "What is Versailles?"

His question seemed to help break the bleak mood. André smiled a little as he replied, "Versailles is one of the world's most glorious palaces, and it was the seat of France's government for many years."

"Uh huh," Zack nodded.

"I could tell you more," the teenager continued, "but you must experience it for yourselves." He pulled out several metro tickets from his pocket.

Katie gulped. "We're going on the metro *alone?*"

André smiled at her. "You will be fine, Katie. I will tell you how to get there and back. It is quite easy from here." He proceeded to explain in detail how to find the right train, where to get out, and how to return. When he offered to draw a map, Zack waved his hand slightly and said, "That's okay. I've got it. I can remember those instructions."

Katie gave him a look.

"What?" he shrugged. "I've got it. Really."

The two kids headed toward the metro with Butterball trotting alongside. Just before leaving, André had tied a new scarf around the puppy's neck that more closely matched Katie's light red beret. Now when people noticed the matching pair, they would usually smile, or nod, or even say something in French that was obviously nice. Katie started walking a little taller.

Zack looked at her and shook his head. "You'd think I was with a movie star."

That made Katie giggle.

When they descended into the same metro station where they had been before, everything looked strange and unfamiliar without André to guide them. They managed to get their tickets into the machine and push through the turnstile, but then a maze of tunnels confronted them.

"There!" Zack said, pointing to a sign which matched André's description.

After going down another flight of steps, they came to the wide platform beside the tracks. Remembering when Butterball's leash had gotten caught, Katie quickly took the puppy into her arms. Bending close to Butterball's ear she said, "We'll never let that happen again, will we!"

The puppy's little black eyes met Katie's, and it certainly looked like Butterball was smiling at her.

When the metro whooshed into the station and came to a stop, they boarded and hurriedly sat down. The car took off, jostling back and forth as it sped along the track. Fortunately, everything seemed uneventful as the train made several stops and people rushed on and off, always seeming to know exactly where they were going. *I sure hope Zack knows where* ***we're*** *going,* she worried after yet another station.

Soon the metro began running above ground alongside the Seine River, and after another stop, Katie started chewing on her fingernail. "Are you *sure* we haven't missed where to get off?" she asked.

"No, it's farther down, I'm sure," Zack said. But Katie could tell by the way he repeatedly looked at a metro map above the car door that he wasn't sure at all.

Finally when the doors opened again, Katie stood up. "We've been on the train too long," she stated. "There's no one left on our car to ask, so I think we should get off and find someone."

"Uh...okay," Zack said, following her out the door, "but I don't think this is right," she heard him mumble.

Once the metro had taken off, Katie set Butterball down. Glancing around, she saw the Seine on one side of them, and a street just above on the other side. "This doesn't look like what André described at all," Katie frowned.

"Oh really?" Zack said, giving her an I-told-you-so look.

"Now what?" she asked.

"Well," Zack said, looking toward the street, "since we're already off the train, we might as well go up there and find someone to give us directions." He started up a sloped stone ramp that led to the avenue just above.

When they reached the top of the incline, they turned left—and stopped dead in their tracks. There on an island in the middle of the Seine River stood a tall, proud lady with her arm raised high, holding a torch. "The Statue of Liberty?" Katie whispered.

When their eyes met, Zack grinned. "Wow, did you get us off at the wrong stop, or what?!"

CHAPTER 9

"I don't get it," Katie said, staring at the Statue of Liberty. She instinctively pulled on Butterball's leash to bring the puppy a little closer.

Beside her she heard Zack start to chuckle. "But the Statue of Liberty is in New York City, on an island."

"Well look!" Katie pointed. "She *is* on an island."

"Yeah, but…well, I don't know," he said, starting to laugh. "But we *can't* be in New York, right?"

Katie's concerned hazel eyes turned to meet his smiling green ones. "There's always the Mr. Gateman thing."

Zack's smile faded as that thought sunk in. "Oh, yeah," he said.

For a moment, neither one spoke while they stared, bewildered, at the regal lady holding a torch. Finally, Zack looked away from the statue and his eyes immediately brightened. "Hey, look!" he called out, pointing.

Katie followed his gaze—and there stood the Eiffel Tower! "Yay!" she giggled with relief. "At least we weren't suddenly sent halfway around the world again."

Zack shook his head. "I don't think New York is halfway around the world from here."

Katie glanced at him. *I'm too happy to argue,* she thought, looking back over toward the proud lady on the island. "But I still want to know why the Statue of Liberty is sitting right there."

"Okay, we'll ask André," Zack replied, "but right now, we need to get to Versailles."

Katie giggled a little. "Yeah, yeah, I know. I got us off at the wrong stop."

Zack just smiled and said, "Let's walk back toward the Eiffel Tower and find someone to help us. We've been in that metro station a couple of times, so we should be able to find our way around." Before Katie could answer, he started off.

I'm not so sure we can find our way around any metro station! she thought, trotting a few steps to catch up.

Along the way they stopped a couple of times to ask people directions, but no one seemed to speak English, so they proceeded on to the metro. As they descended into the station, Katie gulped and lifted Butterball into her arms. Zack hurried over to a metro map on the wall. "Okay," he said, straightening up and pointing, "I think we go that way."

As they headed down a tunnel toward what they hoped was the right train to Versailles, Zack finally found someone who could help them. A young businessman gave them clear directions on the exact number of stops to count and the station name they were looking for.

"Oh yeah," Zack said, "*that's* the station name André told us. Thanks!"

Katie poked him. "Yeah, the one you were sure you didn't need to write down."

When the double-decker train pulled in, Katie and Zack ran to the upper level and took seats facing forward. Katie was setting Butterball at her feet when she heard Zack say, "Look at the ceiling!" Elaborate copies of baroque paintings covered the walls of the car.

The train soon left the crowded city and sailed through villages of steep, dark-roofed houses surrounded by lush greenery. Katie found herself grinning at the beauty of the French countryside. Along the way they carefully counted the stops, and when the doors opened for Versailles, it seemed everyone on the train was going there. "This is perfect," Katie said. "We can just follow the herd."

Zack made a mock sad face and put his hand on his chest. "You don't trust me?"

"You got that right," Katie smiled, punching his arm lightly.

They moved with the throng down a wide sidewalk that took them past all kinds of shops. Each time Katie stopped to look in a store window, Zack would shift from one foot to the other, saying, "Come on, Katie." She pretended not to notice. What she *did* notice was how fashionable all the Parisian women looked—and how she didn't.

They walked a little farther, now far behind the crowd, and turned onto a street that led straight toward the elaborate iron gates of Versailles. Near the entrance, both Katie and Zack stopped, staring wide-eyed at the huge U-shaped complex of four-story buildings standing regally behind a grand golden gate.

"Wow, Katie, it's awesome!" Zack said.

Just then an American-sounding voice beside them said, "Oh, so this is Katie Day! You're finally here!"

Katie whirled to her left to find a middle-aged woman with a walking cast on her foot standing in front of a table. Another woman sat on a plastic folding chair behind the desk, evidently taking registrations for something. *So today is Katie Day? That sounds fun!*

"Um, yes?" Katie responded.

"You're Katie, right?" the woman with the cast said, looking her over. "I just heard the boy call you that."

Katie nodded slowly.

"Great!" the woman smiled warmly, then leaned toward Katie's ear and added, "you're a little younger than we expected, but I hear you're a first-rate rider."

Katie stood dumbfounded, her mouth dropping open slightly.

"Well, come on. You've got your jeans on, so it looks like you're ready to ride." She smiled and added, "I'm sorry it was such short notice. I see you didn't even have time to grab your riding boots."

The woman extended a hand, directing them to walk past the card table. Katie glanced at Zack with wide eyes and mouthed, "What do I do?"

Zack raised his eyebrows and shrugged.

Hobbling in her boot cast, the woman led them over toward a golf cart sitting off to the side. "My name is Olivia," she was saying. "I came to France many years ago, and I've been leading English-speaking horseback tours for ten years now."

We're going riding? Katie wondered, a smile starting to replace her puzzled expression.

Olivia motioned for them to climb into the cart as she continued talking. "But I recently slipped and got the nastiest break, so my doctor insisted I find someone to replace me."

"Uh huh," Katie said, trying hard to figure out what was happening. "I'm sorry about your foot," she added as she picked up Butterball and climbed into the golf cart beside the woman. Zack followed, sandwiching Katie in the middle.

"We thought Nina was all set to ride in my place today," Olivia said, "until she called an hour ago with some emergency, and told us she'd gotten her friend Katie to fill in." Olivia turned to smile at the girl. "And here you are!"

Katie gave her a half smile, still completely perplexed. "Here I am," she echoed.

"So, off we go!" Olivia turned a key, stepped on the pedal, and the cart glided forward along the edge of the street.

They quickly left the palace behind and drove into the countryside surrounding Versailles. Looking around, Katie asked, "Where are we riding?" hoping that wasn't a dumb question.

"All around the palace gardens," Olivia said, indicating the lush area surrounding them. "It's just an hour-long ride, but Françoise simply doesn't feel comfortable speaking English, so she insisted I find someone to help her with this American group." She glanced at Katie. "So you'll be perfect! All you need to do is help them with any riding issues they may have, okay?"

"Sure," Katie said, beginning to grasp this incredible opportunity. *Go, Mr. Gateman!* A grin started across her face.

Just then an elbow jabbed her ribs. "Ooof!" she exhaled, turning to see Zack's eyebrows drawn almost together.

He leaned over and whispered, "What are you doing?"

Katie whispered back, "Riding horses around a royal palace in France!"

Zack shook his head, looking bewildered.

In a very short time the golf cart pulled onto a gravel lane, bounced over a cattle guard, and rolled on through a lush fenced-in pasture with several lofty trees. Stopping next to a large wooden barn, Katie saw a group of Americans mingling and laughing loudly off to the side. In front of the stalls, twelve saddled horses stood tied to a hitching post. One pawed the ground, sending small flurries of dust into the air.

Katie looked them over—and instantly gulped. *They're wearing* ***English*** *saddles!* Her heart began to beat faster. *I don't know how to ride English!*

"Here we are," Olivia was saying as she set the cart's brake. She signaled to a tall, athletic-looking woman by the barn who was wearing proper riding britches, long leather boots, and a black helmet. The woman held a thin switch.

She's going to use that on me when she finds out I can't control the horse! Katie thought, slowly following Zack out of the cart and handing him the puppy.

As Olivia and the woman briefly chatted in French, Katie assumed this must be Françoise. Katie watched as Olivia motioned toward her, and said something that ended in what sounded like "Katie day." Françoise turned to study the girl, looking her over from top to bottom while Olivia went on to explain something else. Katie wanted to run and hide in the barn.

Finally Françoise nodded and turned to untie a horse at the far end. Olivia hobbled back to Katie. "Okay," she said, "we're ready to go. I can at least take care of getting everyone on board while you get used to Tristan." She gestured toward a tall black horse standing near Katie.

Looking at the animal, Katie noticed that not only did he tower above her, but he was also fine-boned and keenly alert. "Tristan," Olivia said, running a tender hand down the horse's sleek neck, "is my full-blood Thoroughbred gelding, so it's a good thing you come highly recommended." She smiled at Katie. "Otherwise he could be a handful…but I'm sure you'll do fine." She straightened his mane and said, "Just keep a light touch on the pelham, and he'll respond like a dream."

I understand that as well as I do French, Katie thought, feeling her heartbeat turn into a full-blown marching band. *What on earth is a pelham? And that horse is way bigger than Tango!*

Katie felt incredibly small and vulnerable as she moved alongside the animal and glanced up—only to discover the situation was getting worse. *How on earth do I get into an English saddle? There's no saddlehorn!*

Katie turned big eyes toward Zack, who was now leaning

against the golf cart, smiling. "Up you go," he said with a big grin, waving his hand toward the lanky gelding.

Olivia removed the rope from Tristan's bridle and held the double reins in her hand. "Here you are, Katie," she said, obviously ready for the girl to climb aboard. "I use a full bridle on Tristan, but you can usually ride on the buckle, because he actually has quite a soft mouth."

Are you speaking English? Katie wanted to scream as she set a hand gingerly on the Thoroughbred's neck. At her touch, Tristan twitched like trying to rid himself of a fly.

Then a thought hit her. *Maybe I'll be given the special ability to ride English! Except...I didn't get it to play the accordion. In fact, I haven't gotten any special abilities on this entire trip....*

Olivia formed a step with her hands, and Katie realized she was getting a leg up. As her heart continued pounding like a rock band, she placed her knee in the woman's hands, and immediately found herself flying through the air. *I'm going to go sailing up and over!* she thought in a panic, grabbing a handful of Tristan's mane.

Managing to land in the slippery, postage-stamp-sized saddle, Katie wasn't about to let go of the horse's hair—until Olivia handed her the set of double reins. *Oh help!* Katie silently pleaded, having no idea how to hold all these strange lines.

Olivia placed her hand on Katie's leg and looked up at the girl. "Go ahead and spend a few minutes with Tristan while I make sure everyone gets mounted, okay?" she said, motioning toward the pasture behind them.

"All right," Katie said, trying hard to sound calm. She glanced down at the ground and bit her lip. *Wow, it's a long way down from here!*

Olivia turned and clumped over to help the tour group—leaving Katie atop the powerful animal. *What should I do now?* she gulped.

Chapter 10

That same Wednesday morning, the Stewart family ventured through a nondescript door into a large, musty room in the heart of Paris. As they stepped into the cavernous space, Veronica Stewart ran a tender hand over her daughter's blonde ponytail. The girl looked up at her mom and wrinkled her nose. "It smells in here," she said, scrunching up her face.

"Shhhh," Mrs. Stewart smiled as she put her finger to her lips.

Russell Stewart glanced over at his wife and said softly, "We don't want to wake up the dead."

She stifled a chuckle and gave him a playful frown.

Stacks of filing cabinets leaned against dark-paneled walls on the right, and the back wall bulged with old documents crammed into tall bookshelves. The clicks of their shoes on the marble floor echoed off the high ceiling like ping pong balls.

"*Excusez-moi,*"[40] Mr. Stewart called out, sounding like a sonic boom in the still air.

A small, wiry man appeared through a door in the far back corner and came striding toward them without making a sound. *Some special skill required for working in this place, no doubt,* Mrs. Stewart thought, watching the thin man silently approach.

He didn't speak until he came right up to Russell Stewart. Standing almost a head lower, he looked over his black-rimmed glasses and said softly, "*Bonjour.*"

"*Bonjour,*" Mr. Stewart answered, discreetly taking a step back. "We were hoping to do a bit of research on some French ancestry. Is this the right place?"

"*Oui, oui, Monsieur,*" he said. "Please follow me."

Their own shoes clicked and clacked as they followed their noiseless leader to one of several long tables across the far end of the room. It wasn't until then that Veronica Stewart noticed a number of people tucked in behind large computer screens lined up like soldiers along the tables. Even the keyboards were evidently required to be soundless.

The man took a seat at a terminal, entered some data, and looked up. "And for whom are we looking?" he asked in clipped, proper English with a French accent.

Mrs. Stewart took a seat beside him and moved the chair a tad closer. "It's my grandfather's French relatives," she said, trying to keep her voice low.

---

40 Pronounced ex-koo-zay-mwah, meaning excuse me

"And what can you tell me about your grandfather?" the man asked, peering at her through thick lenses, making his eyes look oversized.

"Well, during World War II his family lived in a small city outside Paris where they hid some Jews who were running for their lives," she explained. "But the authorities discovered what the family was doing, so they had to flee in the middle of the night."

The man nodded, so she continued. "There were two brothers, eighteen and nineteen years old, and in the darkness of the night, they got separated. They knew they would be killed if they returned home, so they remained in hiding. One soon boarded a boat to America, and the other brother hid in various cities around France." She paused to take a breath. "The one in America was my grandfather."

"I will need a name and the city in France," the stoic man said.

"Yes, of course." Mrs. Stewart drew out a slip of paper from her purse. As she handed it to him she said, "I understand that my grandfather's French surname is quite unusual, so hopefully that will help. So far I've only hit dead ends, since all the records were lost when their town was nearly destroyed in the bombings."

He took the paper, glanced at the name, and merely said, "*Oui*, this is not common." He started to spell out the name as he entered it. "B—R—"

"I certainly hope you can find something," Veronica interrupted, her voice strained. The small man didn't react in the slightest, so she tried to sit quietly as French internet pages began popping up on the computer.

The room resumed its deathly stillness, except when a tiny yawn escaped from Lucy. Then quite unexpectedly the man cried, "Ah!"

Every eye in the room turned toward him. "Did you find something?" Mrs. Stewart asked, moving closer to the screen, though she couldn't read a word of it.

The man's enthusiasm disappeared as quickly as it had come. "No," he said, his hands stopping for a moment. "*Désolé*. That family line moved to Italy, not America." He turned to face Mrs. Stewart with his original expressionless expression. "I am sorry. There is no more information."

Veronica Stewart's shoulders fell. "Well, at least we tried," she said softly, looking up at her husband with eyes that conveyed far more than her words.

The wiry man rose, obviously finished with his research on their behalf. Mrs. Stewart stood to her feet as well and said, "Thank you very much for your help."

The man gave her a slight nod, then turned abruptly and disappeared once again through the far corner door.

"Can we gooooo," Lucy said, pulling gently on her mom's arm.

Mrs. Stewart gave her daughter a tiny smile. "Okay, sweetie. Thank you for coming here with me."

"I'm sorry you didn't find your relatives," Lucy said. "I can't find Butterball, either."

Putting an arm around her daughter's shoulders, Veronica

Stewart ushered her toward the door. "I know, honey. I know," she said. *I feel for you, my sweet girl. I'm concerned about being alone too.*

Lucy looked at her mother with watery eyes. "But Mom, we were so close. Butterball was right there…and we missed her," the girl said in a voice that wrung her mother's heart.

As they moved back out to the warm morning sunshine, Mr. Stewart said in an upbeat tone, "So Luce, we're going to get some ice cream at this gorgeous big palace just outside of town, and then tomorrow morning we'll go to the Jardin d'Acclimatation.[41] That should be lots of fun, riding the roller coasters and the ponies, and seeing the puppet shows, huh?"

Lucy took his hand and walked alongside, but kept her focus on the sidewalk. "Yes, and maybe we'll see Butterball," she said softly.

Katie's palms began to sweat as she held the double reins in one hand, not having a clue as to their proper position. Trying to wipe a hand across her jeans, she saw Françoise watching her.

Closing her eyes, Katie prayed silently, "Lord, if I'm supposed to be on this big horse right now, I'm going to need Your special ability. If not, please get me down!" She took a big breath, and as she let it out…an enormous peace flowed through her body.

---

41 Pronounced Jhahr-dahn dah-clee-mah-tah-see-ohn, meaning Zoological Garden

Immediately rearranging her hands, Katie brought each bottom rein under her hands' fifth fingers and up through her fists, letting the top reins glide between her fourth and fifth fingers. Sitting straight and tall in the saddle, she clucked softly to Tristan, looked toward the field, and shifted her legs ever so slightly to turn the horse into the pasture.

Katie squeezed gently with her calves, and Tristan moved into an easy trot down the field. Without so much as thinking, she automatically began to post, moving up and down according to the horse's stride. *No way!* she thought, a grin spreading across her face. *I'm posting, and it feels completely natural!*

Making a wide circle, Katie connected instantly with her new mount. At the slightest change in her legs, Tristan would move right or left. With the smallest shift in her body, he would effortlessly switch from a trot, to a canter, and back to a walk.

As they began to circle the field in a medium canter, Katie brought her legs forward against the saddle's knee roll, while collecting the horse under her through gentle tension on his bridle. Tristan quickly responded, arching his neck slightly and dropping his chin. Katie could feel the balance of his shoulders and haunches as he brought himself into the bridle. With Katie in perfect alignment over Tristan's supple back, he glided over the ground with grace and efficiency. *Thank you, Lord!* she cried from her heart as she shifted her body and turned Tristan back toward the barn.

When they neared Zack, Katie brought her elbows back just a little and sat deep in the saddle. Tristan came to a stop, his nose about three feet from Zack's amazed face. Katie grinned.

Zack shook his head slowly. "Where'd you learn to ride *English?*"

"Oh...here and there," Katie said off-handedly, feeling a slight twinge over not telling him the *real* reason why she could do these incredible things.

For a moment he just stared at her with puzzled eyes as he reached out to stroke Tristan's face. Finally he said, "So what am I supposed to do while you go riding?"

"How about taking Butterball back to Versailles' main gate and making a sign about her being lost?" Katie suggested.

Right away she could tell he wasn't too excited about that idea. But he nodded, looked down, and said, "Okay. I'll find a way back and meet you there."

"Katie," Olivia called from over by the hitching post, "you look great, and Tristan looks very happy." She gave Katie an approving smile, then motioned toward the eleven riders who were all mounted and beginning to form a line. "And we're ready to go. Françoise will lead the group, and you can follow along at the end in case anyone needs help."

"Okay," Katie said. She glanced back at Zack and Butterball with a grin, then turned Tristan to follow the tour out a side gate.

After riding through a tall archway, the group came to an area Françoise briefly described as having been a farm for Queen Marie Antoinette. They passed several single-story palaces with perfectly manicured gardens and soon rode into a long, tree-lined lane that seemed to stretch to infinity. As they walked alongside delicate daffodils dotting the deep green grass, tourists on foot stopped to gape at them as if they were royalty in a grand parade.

I'm riding where kings and queens rode four hundred years ago! Katie thought, smiling and nodding like a princess.

Trailing the group brought to Katie's mind her time "bringing up the tail" with the drill team near Cassidy Ranch. But rather than racing at breakneck speed to keep up, Tristan and Katie mostly stayed in a fast walk or a leisurely trot. There were moments, however, when one of the tour horses would try to pull out of line, or would nip or kick at another horse. In those times, Katie would give Tristan a quick squeeze with her legs, shift her body slightly forward, and canter up to gently instruct the tour members on how to handle their horses, all while maintaining a perfect seat aboard her powerful Thoroughbred.

Soon the group turned their horses beside a wide canal of crystal blue water. High, impenetrable hedges formed a thick barrier on their left. They walked a short ways and reached a circular clearing where a central fountain shot plumes of water high into the air. And just beyond, at the end of another emerald grass runway, stood a grand fortress on a hill. *The Palace of Versailles!* Katie shook her head. *This is A-MAZ-ING!*

After they had spent some time absorbing the grandeur and snapping photos, Françoise's voice broke into their reverie. "We go back now," she said in her limited English, and the group obediently turned their mounts toward home.

As they started down a path of soft dirt, bordered by trees reaching to the sky, Françoise moved her horse into a slow canter, and each horse behind followed suit. This meant that Tristan, at the end of the line, was able to stretch his long legs into a gallop.

Katie sat forward in the saddle and moved with her steed,

swaying with each stride as if part of the animal's body. Droplets flew from the corners of her eyes as the warm morning breeze blew her hair back. Stifling a "Woo Hoo!" she did think, *I'm gonna give Mr. Gateman the biggest bear hug ever!*

Far too soon the group gathered back at the barn. Katie dismounted quickly, dropping with a soft thud to the ground. After attaching a rope onto Tristan's bridle and giving him an appreciative pat, she hurried over and helped several others dismount. As a middle-aged woman got down, she turned to Katie and said, "Well, thank you so much! I'm glad you were along to help us. It was stunning, wasn't it?"

Katie smiled. "Yes, ma'am, it was gorgeous."

The lady reached over and took Katie's hand, pressing something into her palm as she said, "You are quite an excellent rider, dear."

"Thank you," Katie said, turning a bright shade of pink.

"*Oui*, you are," came an accented voice behind her. Katie whirled around to see Françoise standing nearby. Fortunately she looked happy. "You are…a surprise," she said, searching for the right word. "I will tell Nina 'thank you' for sending us Katie Day."

Katie's eyebrows lowered slightly. "Katie Day?"

Françoise blushed. "Oh, *désolé*, my English so poor. Did I say your name wrong? It is not Katie Day?"

All at once it hit her. *'Katie Day' must be the name of the person they thought was coming! That's why Olivia brought me here—she heard Zack call me Katie!* "Yes," Katie said with a quick smile, "Yes, Katie is right. And it's been wonderful to ride with you."

Françoise nodded and said, "*Merci, et avec toi aussi.*"[42] She then turned back to tending the horses.

Katie shook her head, amazed at the circumstances that had brought all of this about. Walking over to pat Tristan, she looked down to find a ten Euro note in her hand. She giggled as she stuffed it in her pocket and reached up to stroke the black horse's lathered neck. "Well, buddy, thanks for the ride of a lifetime. That was incredible."

"I'm glad you enjoyed it," Olivia's voice said from behind her. "I've been getting glowing reports about you."

Katie turned around. "Really?"

"Oh, absolutely. You were a wonderful help, and you are an amazing rider." She handed Katie an envelope. "Can we call on you again?"

Katie froze for a second, not quite sure how to answer. "Well…sure, just call Katie Day," she said, thinking fast. "That will be great!"

Olivia assured her they would, and then said, "Françoise will take care of cooling and unsaddling the horses. I can get you back to your friend now." She started hobbling toward the golf cart as she said over her shoulder, "I took him and the puppy back to the Versailles entrance gate."

In no time at all, Katie was standing next to Zack and Butterball, waving as her new friend drove away. Then Katie rapidly recounted all her adventures to Zack, explaining why

---

42 Pronounced Mare-see, et ah-vek twa oh-see, meaning "Thank you, and with you too."

she had been asked to help the group.

"Katie Day?" Zack said, his eyes wide. "Go figure." He reached down and patted Butterball, who was wagging furiously at Katie's feet. "That's as crazy as the names people have been inventing for the puppy."

"What do you mean?"

Zack pointed to the cardboard sign beside him. "Olivia helped me make this sign, and the response has been pretty funny."

Katie read the bold letters on the cardboard: LOST PUPPY. MUST KNOW ITS NAME. Katie assumed the French words underneath meant the same thing. "So lots of people have tried to claim her?" she asked hopefully, kneeling down so Butterball could place her furry feet on Katie's legs.

"Well," Zack hesitated, "I mean, she's the cutest thing ever with that red scarf and all, so she's gotten lots of attention. But mostly people just had fun guessing her name." He smiled. "One guy told me she was Mikey, and another guessed Marie Antoinette. I've gotten Fluffy, Rufus, Bebe, Dandelion, Fifi," Zack counted on his fingers, "and best of all…Brutus."

"Brutus!" Katie said, taking the sweet puppy's face into her hands and flipping Butterball's soft ears forward. "You don't look *anything* like a Brutus!"

Butterball slathered Katie's nose.

"Anyhow," Zack said, his smile fading, "we still haven't found her owners."

"Oh." Katie's excitement was instantly deflated. "Well, let's go see if they're inside," she added, standing up.

"Okay," Zack said, handing Butterball's leash to Katie. "And let's get some food. I'm so hungry I could eat a whole pizza by myself."

"You usually do," Katie said with a smirk as Zack bent over and picked up the sign. They walked toward the gate and soon melded into the crowd.

At that exact same moment, near the table where Katie had met Olivia, a couple strolled leisurely toward the palace, each holding the hand of a little blonde girl.

CHAPTER 11

"Let's go to the gardens in the back," Katie suggested as she and Zack entered through a gate into the enormous Versailles estate. "I don't think they'd be too excited about Butterball using the palace rug…if you know what I mean."

Walking behind the palace, their shoes crunched across the wide gravel path that led into a sculpted garden. The scent of freshly cut grass drew Katie's attention to the emerald lawns, topped by hedges forming intricate, symmetrical patterns. All at once, on their right, a fountain burst to life, shooting water sky high and startling Butterball so that she bumped into Katie's leg.

"It's okay, girl," Katie said, kneeling down to reassure the puppy. "It's pretty, isn't it?"

In fact, fountains began to erupt all around them. Classical music rose from speakers hidden throughout the immense gardens, and the aqua plumes looked like water fairies dancing to the melodies. "It's a water ballet," Katie chuckled as she rose to her feet.

"Look at that," Zack pointed toward a circular fountain farther down the gardens. Mythical creatures spouted graceful arches of water that glistened in the afternoon sun. "Let's go down there," he said, immediately heading toward the flight of broad stone steps leading to the spectacle. "Besides," he called over his shoulder, "I'll bet we'll find food in that direction."

Katie picked up the puppy and followed the boy down the steps. When she reached the fountain, Zack was looking right and left. "There's *got* to be someplace to eat!" he said, sounding desperate.

Katie set Butterball back on the gravel. "When I was riding, I saw a café down there by the canal." She indicated an area beyond a long stretch of grass.

"Let's go!" Zack took off before Katie could respond.

Hurrying past enormous walls of thick green hedges, Katie noticed wide paths cutting through them leading to who-knows-where. She tried to glance down one as they walked by. *Everywhere we go, it seems like there are places to get lost.*

Zack rushed on past another gorgeous fountain ringed by tall trees and marble statues as he made a beeline for the restaurant. Katie looked down at Butterball whose stubby legs were moving three times faster than hers. The puppy's pink tongue hung low, sending droplets into the dirt as she tried to keep up. But when she raised her head to look at Katie, the puppy appeared to be grinning. Katie smiled. *Always happy, just like Zack.*

When Katie and the puppy caught up to the boy, he was already seated at a table under a green umbrella, intently perusing the menu. Butterball's "lost" sign leaned up against the table leg.

Katie sat down across from him, and Butterball dropped down under her chair. The puppy's sides heaved up and down. "Butterball can't walk that fast," Katie scolded.

Zack lifted his head and seemed to take a minute to comprehend her words. "Oh. Uh…sorry. I was just starving."

Katie merely shook her head, knowing there was no point in arguing when it had to do with the boy's stomach. She lifted a menu and began to look it over, realizing that she was actually pretty hungry too.

"Wow," Zack said, returning to his study of the choices, "this stuff is expensive!"

Katie glanced at the prices and gave a soft whistle. "Yeah, and we're pretty much out of the money Mr. Gateman left us."

After looking at the menu a moment longer, Katie's eyes suddenly lit up. "Wait a minute!" She dug into her jean's pocket and pulled out the ten Euro note given to her by the woman rider, along with Olivia's envelope. "I forgot to open this," she said, ripping into the paper.

When she produced thirty more Euros, Zack's eyes widened. "Where'd you get all that?"

"From helping with the ride this morning," she smiled. "Pretty awesome, huh?" She met his eyes and grinned. "So how are you going to pay for *your* meal?"

Zack made a face. "You should pay *me* for standing out in

front all morning with a sign about Butterball," he retorted.

Katie smiled. "Yeah, I know. Thanks for doing that. How about we split it?"

"Yes!" Zack said. "Then I *can* have a whole pizza!"

When the waiter came and they asked him for a cup of water for Butterball, he gave them a slight scowl. His face quickly softened, however, when they began ordering large entrees, drinks, and desserts. By the time he had finished recording their choices, they could even detect a faint smile as he said, "You are hungry today."

"Starving!" Zack replied.

While they waited for their food, the warm breeze, the cooling shade, and the beautiful gardens slowly filled Katie with a sense of peace. As she watched tourists renting boats and oars to paddle around the canal's calm waters, she sighed contentedly. "I wish André was here and we could go out in one of those," she said, mostly to herself.

Zack made a snorting noise. "Yeah, I'm sure André would get a kick out of paddling you around in a boat."

Katie stuck her tongue out at him just as their food arrived.

After consuming generous amounts of pizza, baguettes, soft drinks, dessert tarts, and ice cream, Katie sat back and held her stomach. "Ugh. I'm so stuffed!"

Zack smiled. "Feels great, doesn't it?"

"I need to walk around."

Butterball had polished off a full bowl of water and had left no trace of the handouts she'd received, so she seemed ready to go. When Katie and Zack rose from the table, the puppy stretched her front legs out far in front of her and stuck her back end up in the air, making the two kids laugh.

Zack pointed toward some boys throwing a softball back and forth and said, "That looks fun," just as the ball went sailing past the boy nearest them and plopped into the canal.

Like a bullet, Butterball bounded up and dashed toward the water, dragging her leash behind. Zack tried to grab her and missed, so he made a flying leap for her rope—and landed face down in the dirt.

Splash! Butterball did a perfect belly flop into the water.

Zack rushed onto the wooden dock and dropped to his knees, with Katie right beside him. Reaching over the water they called, "Come here, girl. Here, Butterball. Come over here." But the puppy seemed far more interested in going after the softball.

"Her head just went under!" Katie hollered. By now everyone near them was watching the drama unfold.

Stretching out as far as he could, Zack called again, "Come here, Butterball. Come—" *Splash!* He rolled headfirst into the water, sending several ducks squawking angrily into the air.

Quickly resurfacing, Zack flipped thick red hair out of his eyes. In two strokes he reached the puppy, grabbed her around the middle, and held her up with one hand while he swam back to the dock with the other. Then he lifted the soggy little animal safely into Katie's arms.

"Yay, Zack!" she said, hanging on tightly to the wet puppy. "Are you okay, girl?" Katie cooed as she set Butterball on the dock.

In response, the puppy braced her legs and shook her entire

body, sending water flying all over Katie.

"Ugh! I'm all wet!" Katie yelped, falling back on the deck.

Zack, having just hauled his soaking body onto the platform, looked at Katie between dripping locks of hair with eyes that clearly said, *You've got to be kidding.*

They stared at one another for a moment, then both burst out laughing.

As they each sat catching their breath, an official appeared and made sure they were okay. Once he determined they were fine, he sauntered away as if it was just another normal day on the job.

Zack looked at the puppy, who now stood between them with her usual wide-mouthed grin. "You think this is pretty funny, don't you?" he said, wringing water from his shirt.

Katie ran a hand down the puppy's wet fur. "Now why would you do something like that, Butterball?" She peered into the little black eyes.

"She's a retriever," Zack said. "It's in her blood." He shook his mop of red hair like a dog.

"Oh, stop it!" Katie hollered, backing away from Zack's spray. "You're as bad as Butterball!"

After a few minutes they walked over to a fountain where Zack attempted to squeeze more water out of his clothes. Katie gazed down the sculpted stretch of lawn toward Versailles Palace and said, "Look at the view from here! I wish I had a camera."

"Uh huh," Zack responded without glancing up. "How 'bout if we work our way back up there through these groves?" He motioned toward a path to his left leading into the high hedge walls. "Then the whole world won't see me looking like a drowned rat."

"Okay," she said, "but let's not get lost."

Following Zack through the tall shrubbery, they came into a large circular area with a sign that read *Bosquet de l'Encelade.*[43] "Wow," Zack said, staring at the enormous gold statue in the middle of the circle. A man, buried from the waist down by a pile of rocks, reached toward heaven as he struggled to rise. "Looks like he got buried alive."

Katie scrunched up her nose and turned to look around. "Hey, those are cute," she said, stepping onto a grassy area beside several shrubs that were shaped like teapots, as tall as her.

"*Descendez de l'herbe!*" a voice shouted from nearby.

Katie leaped off the thick grass onto the dirt path and whirled around to see a stern guard off to her left, pointing at her feet. She didn't need a translator to know what he'd just said. "But I wasn't on the grass," she replied sweetly, giving an innocent shrug.

The instant the words were out of her mouth, a roar of thunder shattered the air so violently that it shook the ground beneath Katie's feet!

"Lucy, look at Versailles' chapel," Veronica Stewart said, putting an arm around the girl and bringing her forward to peer through the iron bars. "Look how elegant and tasteful this

43 Pronounced Boe-skay deh lan-sell-ahd, meaning Grove of Enceladus, a giant from Greek mythology

is," she pointed toward the decorative marble arches supporting a second story of tall Corinthian columns. "See how they march all the way up to that magnificent pipe organ?"

Her daughter gazed through the barrier. "Uh huh, it's pretty."

"Let's keep going, Ronni," Mr. Stewart said from behind them.

As the family worked their way through the palace into the kings' and queens' bedrooms, Veronica Stewart shook her head. "All this gold and marble and crystal…" she met her husband's eyes, "it's a bit overwhelming."

They moved quickly through the rest of the rooms and came to a long hall lined with tall statues of men in military uniforms. Lucy stopped in front of a marble soldier who pointed urgently to the left with his right arm across his chest. "Look, Dad," she giggled, "he's saying, 'That way for ice cream.'"

Mr. Stewart laughed and took his daughter's hand. "Well, we'd better do what the man says."

As they stepped outside onto the hard-packed gravel path, Lucy looked at her father. "Your map said the ice cream was *way* down there," she pointed past a large fountain toward the long canal in the distance.

"So let's go," Mr. Stewart smiled.

After walking past the fountain and alongside tall, thick hedges, they finally drew closer to the canal. Lucy began pulling on her dad's hand and pointing with her other arm. "There it is! I see the restaurant," she said.

At that moment, a loud, thunderous rumble shook the ground.

CHAPTER 12

Katie felt like she jumped a mile when the explosive roar split the air. She turned toward Zack with enormous eyes, and saw that he looked as startled as her. But when music and dialogue started coming from some speakers around the statue, Katie realized that the thunder had only been part of a recording.

Putting her hand over her heart, she gasped, "I thought God was about to strike me with lightning because I said I wasn't on the grass!"

Zack met her eyes and said, "Maybe He should have."

She made a face at him, but her recent conversation with André about honesty instantly came to mind again. *And when I was stuck on the Notre Dame balcony, I told God I'd try to do better,* she grimaced. *Well, at least this wasn't a big deal.*

"Come on, Katie," Zack waved his arm. "Let's keep going."

As they continued winding their way through various hedge groves, Katie's heart grew heavier. When they emerged close to the royal house, she pulled Mr. Gateman's note from her jeans and reread it for the hundredth time. Her feet dragged, raising little clouds of dust as she walked slowly toward the building.

"What's wrong?" Zack asked.

She shook her head. "I just don't get what Mr. Gateman wants me to do," she sighed. "Am I supposed to learn something that will help us find Butterball's owners?"

Zack bent down and patted the puppy. "I don't know…but it's Wednesday, and…" his voice trailed off.

Katie nodded slowly. "We haven't seen the family here, and now we need to head back. And on Friday she'll have to go to the…the pound." Katie could barely say the word. "I can't stand to even think about that."

Zack glanced up at her. "Maybe André's Uncle Pierre will take her."

"That's possible. But André said he wasn't very nice."

With a shrug Zack said, "He can't be that bad. Besides, it's better than the pound." He gave her a slight smile. "And we still have tomorrow."

"But we don't even know where the family might be tomorrow," Katie said. "They were supposed to be *here* today."

Zack thought for a second, still stroking Butterball's fur. "Hey, if we haven't found the owners by tomorrow afternoon, maybe André could play his accordion and we could advertise a free puppy."

Katie met his eyes. "Yeah, maybe."

"All we can do is keep praying, Katie," Zack said, rising to his feet. "God can put us in the right place."

She looked away and nodded. "Let's go," she said, barely loud enough for Zack to hear.

They didn't talk too much on the train ride home, until a man boarded with an accordion. His happy music and big, toothy smile helped cheer Katie so that she soon found herself thinking, *Maybe we **can** advertise Butterball tomorrow if we can't find her real family.* By the time they got off the train and walked back to André's house, Katie felt better.

As they started up the bakery's winding staircase, Katie could hear André and his mom talking on the first level. They found Madame Boulanger in the kitchen and André sitting at the dining room table looking at some books. Soft voices from a television floated around the living room wall, and Katie guessed Monsieur Boulanger was resting back there after a long day at the bakery.

"*Bonjour*," Madame Boulanger said cheerfully. "Welcome home."

"How was your time?" André asked, glancing down at the puppy. "I see we still have our friend with us."

"I'm sure glad she has a nametag," Zack said. "Lots of people tried to guess her name, but no one even got close." He smiled. "Someone even called her *Brutus!*"

"Is that right?" André looked over at Katie.

"Katie wasn't there," Zack said.

André's eyebrows shot up as he looked at the girl. "Where were you?"

Katie proceeded to tell them about being mistaken for

someone named Katie Day, and how she ended up riding as a tour guide around the grounds of Versailles. As her story unfolded, Madame Boulanger stopped cooking and stood with her mouth ajar. When Katie finished, the lady shook her head and said, "*Incroyable!*"

"Oh, and guess what else happened to us," Katie said. "We made a slight mistake on the way to Versailles and got off by the Statue of Liberty." She turned toward André. "But what is the Statue of Liberty doing in the Seine River?"

André laughed. "Do not worry, Katie, your statue is still standing in New York City." He looked over at his mom, who smiled and resumed clattering pans and dishes. "The one you saw is about one-tenth the size of Lady Liberty in America," André explained. "Bartholdi, the sculptor, created the smaller version as a model for yours."

Katie giggled and said, "When we saw it, I thought for a second we'd gotten transported to New York City." As soon as the words were out of her mouth, she realized the implication of what she'd said and glanced urgently at Zack.

But André and his mom didn't seem to notice anything strange. Instead, André turned toward the books in front of him. "When I had a break today, Katie, I was able to find *30 Days with God* in English."

"Perfect!" She took a seat beside him while Zack sat down across from them.

André scooted a booklet over to Zack and said, "I got you one too."

"Hey, thanks!" Zack immediately opened it.

André flipped to a page in Katie's booklet. "It is exactly like mine," he said, "only not in French." He pointed to the top of the page. "See, here is the Bible verse for the day, and then just below it is a short paragraph explaining what you read. Then there is a section to help you apply it to your life."

"What are these dog-eared pages?" she asked, noticing several with the corners turned down.

André smiled. "I did that. I thought you might want to start there…to help with what we talked about."

Katie's face started to feel warm. She glanced up to see if Madame Boulanger reacted, but when the woman went right on cooking, Katie guessed that André hadn't told her anything about the fibs.

Continuing, André said, "Katie, remember how we talked about the importance of feeding our new spiritual nature?"

She nodded. "Whatever you feed, grows."

"That is right," André smiled. "And the Bible is the best food, because it is God speaking to us."

Katie smiled. "Zack's mom told me, 'whatever God says to us, we can always trust to be right.'"

"*Oui,*" Madame Boulanger spoke up from the kitchen, "no other book in the world can claim that. And do you know *why* we can always trust the Scriptures, Katie?" she asked.

The girl shook her head.

Madame stopped cooking and placed her mitted hands on the counter. "Katie, the Bible is made up of sixty-six books, written in three languages, on three continents, over a period of 1,500 years."

Katie's eyes stayed fastened on the woman.

Taking a breath, Madame continued. "These books were written by many authors, covering thousands of topics. And that is important to know because here is the astounding part—every single thing they wrote agrees!"

Katie tried hard to absorb all this information. "I…I'm not sure I get it," she said.

André jumped in. "Think of it like this," he said. "You have two older brothers, *oui?*"

Katie nodded and made a face.

André smiled. "Do you agree on everything?"

"No way!" she said. "We hardly *ever* agree!"

André nodded. "*Exactement.* And that is true of us all. It is difficult to agree. Yet God used around forty writers from many different places—and *everything* they wrote agrees perfectly." He paused. "The only way for that to happen is for God to have written *through* them."

Katie frowned. "So…how did *God* write it if men actually did the writing?"

"Let me show you this," André said, opening the Bible on the table in front of him. When he found the right page, he said, "Here is what the Apostle Paul wrote. 'All Scripture is inspired by God and is useful to teach us what is true and to make us realize what is wrong in our lives.'"[44] He looked at Katie. "It means God put the ideas and words into the writers' minds. When the men wrote, their own personalities came through, but

44 2 Timothy 3:16

the words are one hundred percent what God wanted, and are always true and right."

Katie nodded. "So it's all really God's words, but He used men's hands to put it down?"

"*Oui.* And the verse goes on to say that the Scriptures also 'make us realize what is wrong in our lives.'"

At hearing those words, Katie cringed as she thought about how many times she had recently done or said things that were wrong. "I get it," she nodded.

André pushed the small Bible study booklet toward her and smiled. "I hope you enjoy this as much as I have."

She picked up the book and met his eyes. "Thanks so much. I know I will."

Right then Madame Boulanger called out, "Dinner!"

The soft chatter of the television stopped, and Monsieur Boulanger appeared from around the wall. Everyone took a seat as André's mother brought out platters from the kitchen. After they prayed and started to eat, Madame Boulanger smiled at Katie and Zack and said, "So what did you think of our little palace today?"

"That place is awesome!" Katie replied.

Zack nodded enthusiastically while he chewed, then said, "It was fun to walk around, and Butterball got lots of attention." He swallowed and added, "Everyone noticed Katie's and Butterball's matching hat and scarf."

Katie grinned at André and said, "Yeah, I love that beret." Then she turned to Madame Boulanger. "But I don't feel very stylish around all the fancy Paris girls."

"Oooh!" the lady instantly perked up. "We must accessorize!" She smiled. "I will help you after dinner, Katie."

"Great!" Katie said, not too sure what that meant, exactly.

All at once Zack exclaimed, "Yum!" Katie turned to see him reaching for another palm-sized round shell sitting in a shallow dish. She watched as he used a small pronged fork to pry out some soft meat, then he dipped the morsel in a buttery sauce and popped it in his mouth.

Katie picked up the little fork beside her plate to try it while Zack was already at work digging out another one. "These are good!" he exclaimed.

André must have noticed Katie struggling with the tiny fork, because he said, "Like this, Katie." He lifted a shell and inserted his prong slowly. Katie watched, then tried to duplicate his actions. In her attempt to hold the slippery shell while digging inside, it slid through her fingers and shot across the table—landing on the edge of Monsieur Boulanger's plate!

Katie caught her breath and turned big eyes toward the man.

Monsieur Boulanger looked up at Katie with a frown, but before he could speak, his wife started to laugh. Then André joined in, along with Zack. Katie watched as the corners of the stern man's mouth slowly began to curve upward, until a gentle sort of chuckle came from his throat. Katie exhaled.

"Not quite right," he said, picking up the shell and handing it back across the table to her.

Katie giggled. "Okay, I can do this. Let me try again." This time she popped out the soft meat and dipped it into the buttery sauce. As she chewed the morsel, warm butter ran down her throat. "This *is* good," she said. "What is it?"

"Escargot,"[45] André replied beside her. "You call them snails."

Katie stopped chewing. She looked across the table at Madame and Monsieur…and knew there was only one option. Closing her eyes, she swallowed hard. *Conch in the Bahamas, escargot in Paris…snails seem to be following me around the world!* She hoped the little critter would stay down.

The rest of dinner was a feast of breaded chicken with some sort of spinach that actually tasted great, followed by various cheeses. As Katie finished off a chocolate éclair, she remembered all they had eaten at lunch. *They're going to call* ***me*** *Butterball when I get home!* she thought, leaning back contentedly in her chair.

Right after the meal, Madame Boulanger disappeared into her room, reemerging with a red patterned scarf to go with Katie's beret, as well as a very large bag. The woman handed Katie the oversized purse, then arranged the scarf around her neck. Stepping back, Madame looked her over and said, "*Bien*. Now you look French."

When Katie went to her room, Zack followed along and sat on her floor for a few minutes, playing with Butterball. They talked about what Madame Boulanger and André had told them concerning the trustworthiness of the Bible and about spending time with God, until Katie yawned and said, "Well…I'm pretty tired."

Zack patted the puppy for a moment, then glanced up at

45 Pronounced es-car-go

her. "Oh, okay," he said, rising to his feet and heading toward the door. "See ya tomorrow."

Throughout the night, Katie dreamed of leading Butterball with a diamond-studded leash along the Parisian boulevards while people stared in admiration. When she awoke the next morning, however, Butterball the Star was once again Butterball the Bedhog. Katie slid the puppy across the bed and said sternly, "I'm going to rename you Butterhog if you don't quit cramming me against the wall!"

Rolling out of bed, Katie felt—what was it?—grumpy. *Probably because it's Thursday and we're running out of time.* Even the beautiful soprano voice down the street failed to bring a smile to her face.

She walked over to the dresser and frowned at herself in the mirror. Then her eyes fell on the booklet André had given her. Picking it up, Katie flipped through a few pages, stopping at the first one with a dog-eared corner. It said:

Read:
Jesus told His disciples, "*He who is faithful in a very little thing is faithful also in much; and he who is unrighteous in a very little thing is unrighteous also in much*" (Luke 16:10 NASB)

Learn:
Wait a minute! Did I just read that right? I mean, we all like to be noticed and rewarded for being faithful in the little things—and God **does** bless us greatly. But what's that second part? "*He who is unrighteous in a very little thing is unrighteous also in much.*" Ouch! In other words,

in God's eyes the little things **are** important, because if I'm not pleasing Him in the little stuff, it shows that I'm not willing to obey Him in every part of my life. So God says it's just as important to be faithful in the small areas of life as the big.

Apply:

Is there anything in my life, even a "little" thing, where I haven't been pleasing to God? If so, I need to confess that to Him right now, and ask Him to help me be faithful in every word and action today.

Those words pierced Katie's heart like a sword. *I haven't been honest so many times lately, and I keep saying that it's no big deal. But God says it's a* ***big*** *deal…because the little things show what I'm really like.*

Katie sat down on the bed next to Butterball and put a hand on the puppy. "Oh Butterball, I don't want to be someone who's unrighteous…even in the little things."

The puppy looked up at her with gentle black eyes and thumped her tail against the sheets.

Katie dropped her head, clasped both hands in her lap, and closed her eyes. Taking a big breath she said, "Dear God, I'm so sorry for all the lies I've told. And I'm sorry I keep saying they're no big deal, because You say they *are* a big deal. God, I really want to please You." She paused. "Please Lord, help me do what's right in everything…especially the stuff I say."

Butterball wiggled closer and dropped her head on Katie's leg. Katie opened her eyes and rubbed behind the puppy's floppy ears. "And please, please God," she added, "help us find

Butterball's family today so she doesn't have to go to the pound."

For a few minutes the only sounds in Katie's room were car horns and chattering people from the street below. When she finally set the puppy on the floor and stood up, a smile broke across her face. "Hey, I don't feel grumpy anymore!" she said out loud, amazed by the rapid change. "I wonder if this is part of what Mr. Gateman said I should learn here."

Katie found herself humming as she got cleaned up and dressed. When she arrived in the kitchen, she found Zack there. He had already eaten and was waiting for her. "Hi!" she said.

He smiled a little. "You seem happy."

She grinned. "Yeah."

"Well," Zack said in a soft voice, "I don't think you're going to be too happy about this."

Katie's heart skipped a beat. *That doesn't sound good.* "What?" she asked, her smile fading.

"I just found out that André's uncle is coming to town this morning, and we're all going out for coffee…and he wants us to bring Butterball."

"What? But we're supposed to have one more day left to find her family!" Katie objected. "I want Butterball returned to that sweet little girl, not sent off to some grouchy uncle who isn't very nice."

Zack gave a slight shrug. "But don't you think it's better than taking her to the pound?"

Katie looked out the kitchen window. "I hope so," she mumbled, *but something about this just doesn't feel right.*

CHAPTER 13

"*Allons-y!*[46] Let's go!" Madame Boulanger's voice called up the stairs.

For a moment Katie hesitated, then hurried back up to her bedroom to grab the cute accessories from Madame Boulanger. *What I'd really like to do is grab Butterball and go hide in one of those groves at Versailles.* Picking up the puppy, she whispered, "Lord, please help Butterball."

When Katie met the family in the courtyard, she wanted to talk to André and at least plead for one more day to look for the little girl; but he was over by the passage doorway, opening it for someone.

At that instant, a man even more stout-chested than

46 Pronounced Ahl-lown-zee

Monsieur Boulanger burst through the door and grabbed André's shoulders, kissing him brusquely on both cheeks. Katie gulped. *Uncle Pierre!* Then the man took three enormous strides over to his brother and embraced him.

"Jacques!" Uncle Pierre said loudly, going through the motions again, even rougher than before.

That scruffy beard must feel like an iron scrub brush! Katie instinctively held the puppy tightly and eased back into the shadows of the courtyard. *I wish we could somehow disappear,* she thought as Zack quickly joined her.

Next, Uncle Pierre turned his attention to Madame Boulanger. As the gruff giant reached toward the slight woman, Katie feared he might crush her with his large hands. But he held her lightly and said, "Monique Brineaux," blowing kisses past both of her cheeks.

The adults spoke rapidly to one another in French, until Monsieur Boulanger motioned over toward Katie and Zack, saying their names. Uncle Pierre looked at them without so much as a nod of greeting. Instead, his eyes fell on Butterball.

Katie tried to swallow, but her throat felt constricted. When the hulk took several steps toward her, she wanted to run, but found she couldn't move. "*C'est donc mon nouveau chien!*" he bellowed, reaching out and roughing Butterball's head like he was screwing on a faucet. "*Il n'est pas encore assez grand pour manger!*" he added loudly, then threw his head back and roared a laugh that raked across Katie's bones.

As the giant walked back over toward his brother, André appeared behind Katie. "Do not let him frighten you," he whispered in her ear. "He is only teasing."

Like I really know what he said! "What did he say?" she asked urgently.

"Well..." André hesitated, "he said, 'So this is my new dog.'"

Katie turned to André with accusing eyes. "What *else* did he say?"

André looked down and mumbled, "He said, 'She is not even big enough to eat yet.'"

Katie gasped. *That monstrous man is way* ***worse*** *than André told us!*

André grabbed her arm and pulled her over toward the bakery door. "Katie," he said firmly, "Pierre says things to annoy people. He is loud and crude and...not like a Frenchman at all. He may not be very kind to animals, but he would not eat a dog. I promise."

She looked at him skeptically, but didn't have time to beg that Butterball be spared from this horrible fate, because the Boulangers were heading out the passage. "*Allons-y, André!*" his mother called.

Katie and Zack trailed the group as they all headed toward the Pont Saint-Louis. Katie felt like she was carrying the poor puppy off to be sacrificed as she held the warm bundle tightly. Leaning toward Zack she whispered, "That man is *terrible!* We can't let Butterball go to him!" She looked at the boy. "What if we make a run for it?"

Zack's eyes widened. "We can't do that! Besides, where would we hide in Paris?"

I know a bunch of places! Katie thought, biting her lip.

When they arrived at the corner café, all the adults crowded around one small outdoor table, with Zack, Katie, and André huddled around the table beside them. Katie dropped her big handbag, then set Butterball down. To her horror, the puppy trotted straight over to Uncle Pierre!

The hulk immediately bent down, lifted the puppy up around her middle, and held her directly in front of his unshaven face. Katie held her breath. He said something to her, then set her back on the sidewalk and resumed talking with the others.

Katie whirled toward André. "What did he say?" she demanded.

André shrugged. "He just said that he is looking forward to introducing her around the farm tomorrow."

Katie did a double-take. "Wait a minute…tomorrow? So he's not taking her this morning?"

"No, no," André shook his head. "Pierre is just passing through town today to pick up some things. He decided he wants the puppy, but said his car is too full to take her now. My parents are not very happy about the dog going to him, but what can they do?" André shrugged helplessly. "Papa said we could drive down to his farm south of here tomorrow, since the bakery will be closed."

Katie slumped back hard against her chair and blew out her lips. It felt like Butterball had just been given a reprieve from prison—at least for a day. "Boy, is that the best news, or what?" she said, flipping her scarf back as she met Zack's eyes. "Now we've absolutely *got* to find that little girl today!"

"Definitely!" Zack said, eyeing Uncle Pierre with a look Katie had never seen before.

"*Oui*, I agree," André whispered. "I have seen how he treats his own dog." He paused. "But first we need to be polite and remain here a little longer."

After the waiter had taken the adults' orders, he turned toward André. "*Et vous?*"[47] he asked.

André ordered café, then looked at Katie. "What would you like?"

"Well...I didn't have time for breakfast," she said, feeling her stomach growl at the mention of food, "so could I get a roll and some orange juice, or something like that?"

André ordered for her, then turned to Zack. The boy grinned at him and said, "I'll have what you're having."

"You want café, my young friend?" André asked, his eyebrows arching slightly.

Katie gave Zack a look. "You don't drink coffee."

Zack kept his eyes on André. "All cowboys drink coffee. My Dad drinks it all the time."

André smiled slightly, looked at the waiter, and nodded toward Zack. "Okay, *deux* cafés."[48]

While they waited, Katie felt such an incredible sense of relief at the turn of events that she chattered happily. When their order came, she eagerly bit into the soft, buttery croissant

---

47 Pronounced Ā (long a sound) voo, meaning "And you?"

48 Pronounced der cah-fay, meaning two coffees

André had gotten her. She happened to look up in time to see Zack take a swallow from his tiny cup of very black coffee. Right away she could tell he was trying hard not to make a face as he swallowed.

"So tough cowboy, how's the coffee?" Katie asked with a grin.

Zack nodded. "Good," he squeaked, about an octave higher than normal, which made them all laugh.

Soon André received permission from his father for the three youths to leave. Zack leaped up like a jack rabbit. Uncle Pierre lumbered around in his chair to look down at Butterball and said something in a loud voice, making Katie cringe even though she didn't understand it.

André just smiled politely and motioned for Katie and Zack to follow him across the bridge. Katie was more than happy to leave. "What'd he say?" she asked as they started across the Pont Saint-Louis.

André looked away. "Just something typical. He said to be sure and keep Butterball safe, because he has plans for her."

Katie gulped. "What does *that* mean?"

André shook his head. "Forget it. We just need to find her family."

Zack started talking more than Katie had ever heard, carrying on about finding the puppy's owners, and how the Cassidy's dog, Toby, had a great life on the ranch, and how it was a mystery that Katie could ride English, and on and on.

Finally Katie turned to him and said, "What's wrong with you? You're jabbering nonstop!"

André put a hand on the boy's shoulder and said, "I am afraid you are a little—what do you call it?—'wired' from that strong café, *mon ami.*"[49]

Katie giggled. "Wired with enough energy to light up New York!"

"It will wear off…eventually," André said as Zack began jumping on and off a low wall next to the sidewalk.

Starting past Notre Dame, Katie said, "Where should we go today, since we don't know where the family will be?"

André thought for a moment. "Women love perfume, so I suggest we try the Fragonard Perfumery first, then we will go to the Louvre[50] Museum. Every tourist goes there."

While they walked, André turned to Katie and said, "France is the perfume capital of the world. Here, almost all women wear perfume, and a great number of men wear cologne."

Zack shook his head but finally held his tongue. Katie smiled, because she knew he was thinking that no cowboy would ever be caught dead wearing perfume.

When they came to a flower shop, Katie paused to admire the radiant blooms filling the air with their delicate fragrances. Lavender and white orchids, cyclamens of brilliant pink and coral, azaleas of deep salmon, and roses of every color crowded the tables in front of the shop. "Mmmm," she breathed in, "this is better than any perfume from a bottle."

All of a sudden a woman wearing an apron came hurrying

---

49 Pronounced mohn a-mee, meaning my friend

50 Pronounced Loov

toward her waving a large pair of garden clippers. She was yelling something in French and looking just past Katie toward the sidewalk. Katie glanced down in time to see Butterball rising up from a squatting position in a flatbed of herbs. "Go away!" the woman switched to English. "Out! Take your dog away!" she pointed the clippers menacingly at the puppy.

"But she—" Katie was about to say Butterball hadn't wet on the herbs when she stopped midsentence. "*And he who is unrighteous in a very little thing is unrighteous also in much*" flashed across her mind like a neon sign. "Sorry!" Katie called, hurriedly stepping away from the shop, dragging Butterball with her.

Zack and André were already trotting down the street. When she caught them, they all stopped to laugh. Zack looked at Katie and said, "I thought she was coming after *you!*"

"Me too!" Katie replied, looking down at Butterball whose tongue hung out from their dash down the lane. Bending down to give the puppy a pat, she said, "That woman wasn't very happy about you watering her garden, huh, girl?"

Butterball gave a sharp little bark and looked like she was laughing with them.

Continuing on, they passed several long wooden sale racks overflowing with fruits and vegetables, then came to an open plaza in front of a church. "Look!" Katie said, pointing toward an enormous chalk drawing in the center of the plaza floor. A tall masted ship sailed across cobalt waters toward a sunset of vivid oranges and pinks. Katie noticed the man crouching in the picture's far corner, drawing intently with blue chalk.

"They do it for tips," André explained, "like when I play *accordéon*."

"He's good," Zack said as he swung around a lightpole near the drawing. "Yeah, really good. That's an excellent ship. I like it. Wish I could draw like that. I can sorta draw a horse. Yup, I like that drawing a lot."

Katie looked at André. "When does the caffeine wear off?"

He just shrugged.

As they walked on, Katie constantly watched for an American family with a blonde girl. Soon they turned down a passageway between buildings and arrived in a small courtyard. Through tall glass doors Katie could see inside Fragonard Perfumery where hundreds of golden bottles lined the shelves, and tables overflowed with colorful boxes and various canisters. But what really filled the store was people. *Lots* of people. "It's so crowded," she said, instinctively picking up Butterball.

"There are many tourists today," André nodded. "They will not want the puppy inside, so I will stay out here with her while you two go in."

Zack immediately turned toward André. "I can stay with you!"

But André motioned with his hand for the boy to go on inside.

Katie started through the door, and instantly the delicate bouquet of flower scents made her smile. Behind her she heard Zack mumble, "It should be called a *pew*fermery."

They moved into the store and tried to look for Butterball's family, but it was hard to see through the crush of people. Zack squeezed between two large women to stand beside Katie. "Let's go over by the counter," he suggested. "At least there we won't be so squished."

They maneuvered their way to one side of the shop and were able to crowd against a counter lined with brightly colored canisters and bottles.

"Hey, look at this," Zack said, lifting up a tiny silver container. "It's got a horseshoe on it." He twisted open the lid and cautiously took a sniff. "Still smells like perfume," he winced, turning his head away.

In a flash a woman appeared in front of Zack. "May I help you?" she asked sweetly.

Zack quickly set the small container down. "No, thank you," he answered politely.

The clerk smiled. "That is a 'perfume solid,' just for men. It is not as concentrated as the spray perfume."

Katie grinned at him. "Then you should definitely go for the spray," she said.

Zack looked at her with threatening eyes as the clerk hurried to pick up a tall silver bottle nearby. "Would you like to try the scent?" she asked, holding up a thin strip of paper on which to spray the cologne.

At that moment, a woman behind Katie bumped hard into her, throwing her against Zack, who fell forward and ended up with the full blast of perfume down the front of his shirt. "Yuck!" he yelled so loud that every head in the store turned his way.

Chapter 14

Looking utterly horrified, Zack quickly righted himself and began wiping his hands down his shirt, only spreading the perfume more thoroughly. "It's everywhere!" he moaned.

"Oh! *Je suis désolé!*" the clerk apologized. "I am so terribly sorry!"

Katie watched Zack's face contort as he held his arms out away from his sides. "Gag! I smell like...*flowers!*" He wrinkled his nose, making his freckles blend together.

She couldn't help but giggle, and other customers began to chuckle as well.

"It's not funny!" Zack snapped, his face beginning to match the color of his bright red hair.

She tried putting a hand over her mouth, but it didn't seem to help.

"I don't believe this," he muttered, starting toward the door. Katie followed a little ways behind.

When they reached André, the teenager smiled and said, "Did you find the puppy's—" he stopped, a puzzled look crossing his face. "Zack, did you buy some cologne?"

Zack's head dropped as Katie's giggles started all over again. "He really liked the perfumes," she said.

Just then Butterball sneezed. Then she sneezed again...and again. Katie picked the puppy up and moved several feet away from Zack as she said, "I think Butterball is allergic to your brand."

André looked at Katie with questioning eyes, so she related all that had happened, ending with, "I didn't *mean* to knock him into the clerk while she was spraying the cologne...but it was definitely funny. You should have seen his face."

Zack looked up with pleading eyes. "What am I going to do, André?" He sounded desperate. "I can't walk around like *this!*"

André smiled, and Katie thought for sure it looked like he was trying not to laugh. "I'm afraid it will take some time to wear off, *mon ami*," he said, shaking his head. "But remember, half of all men in France wear cologne, so it is not unusual."

"But they don't wear a whole bottle at once. I smell like an entire flower shop!"

Katie looked at André. "It wasn't really an entire bottle," she grinned.

Her smile faded quickly, however, as she remembered their urgent time limit. Stepping around Zack and moving toward the passageway she said, "Well, unfortunately we don't have time to go home, because we need to get to the Louvre and find the family."

Butterball sneezed again.

"Great," Zack mumbled, slowly turning to follow Katie. The strength of the perfume seemed to have overpowered the effects of the morning coffee.

As they made their way toward the museum, a few pedestrians turned to look at the sweet-smelling boy, then continued past with a smile. Katie had to stay several paces ahead, because whenever Butterball got near Zack, the puppy would sneeze.

After walking for a while, they arrived at a tall arched monument next to a park. André was just starting to explain something about the large structure when his cell phone rang. He spoke briefly to someone, then jammed the phone into his jeans and turned to Zack and Katie with the same sad eyes she had seen before. "That was my father," he said. "I have to return to the bakery."

"André," Katie said slowly, not sure if she should ask what was on her mind. "You talked with me about the importance of being honest, right?"

He nodded.

"Well…shouldn't you be honest with your dad about what you really want to do?"

Instead of responding right away, André stared at the ground for a moment. When he finally looked up he said, "Yes, that is true, Katie. But…it must be the right time." He paused. "I will pray for that time."

She gave him a gentle smile.

André turned and led them just beyond the monument into a large courtyard. An imposing three-story U-shaped building surrounded them. In the courtyard, lots of people relaxed on the wide ledge around a water fountain. Pointing toward a long line waiting to enter a glass pyramid, André said, "That is the main way into the Louvre. So if you sit here on the ledge, hopefully you will see Butterball's owners."

"There are other entrances?" Katie asked.

"*Oui*," André nodded, "there are three more entrances, some underground. But this is where the majority of tourists come. And you are not allowed to take the puppy in, so this is the best place for you."

"What's inside the Louvre?" Zack asked, looking at the enormous stone building around them.

"It was originally a fortress," André explained, "then the palace of the king. But Louis the Fourteenth moved the entire royal court out to Versailles, and now the Louvre is one of the largest museums in the world. Inside are Michelangelo sculptures, famous paintings like the *Mona Lisa*, jewels, mummies… everything imaginable from history."

"Mummies!" Zack's eyes lit up. "Awesome!"

Katie looked at him and grinned. "Yeah, you could probably wake them up with that smell."

Zack made a face.

"Okay, I must go," André said. "I will see you tonight. And…" he paused and dug into his pocket, "I would like to give you some money for lunch and snacks. It is my gift."

"Thanks!" Zack reached for the money.

Keeping his eyes on the boy, André handed the bills over to Katie. "I think it is probably better if she goes to get the food, *n'est-ce pas*?"[51]

Zack looked chagrined. "Yeah, I guess so," he said, kicking the courtyard's stone surface with his tennis shoe.

André started to leave, then looked back at Katie. "I will pray that you find Butterball's owners."

"Yes, please keep praying," Katie said, feeling again a great sense of urgency.

As the teenager walked away, Zack hopped up on the ledge and said, "This looks like a good spot."

Scooping up Butterball, Katie sat down next to the boy. *Choo!* Butterball sneezed.

"Oops," Katie said, meeting Zack's eyes. "Guess we'd better slide down a little."

Zack rolled his eyes, then said, "Why don't you go get us something to eat?"

Katie sighed. "Okay. But you'd better look really hard for the family."

"I will, I will," he said, motioning for her to go.

Katie returned shortly with sandwiches, drinks, and some water for the puppy. She couldn't think of much to talk about, so she just ate quietly and watched the crowd while Butterball curled up at her feet and slept. Occasionally someone would sit down between her and Zack, then turn quickly to look at the

---

51 Pronounced ness pah, meaning "it is not?" or "isn't it?"

boy. Invariably they would act like they'd forgotten something and leave. After the third occurrence, Katie smiled at him and said, "You're sure popular."

Zack just looked humiliated.

Several hours slowly ticked by. Finally, Katie stood up and said, "This isn't working."

"What else can we do?" Zack shrugged.

"We can go inside," she motioned toward the line snaking its way into the large glass pyramid.

"We can't take Butterball in there," Zack protested. "Besides, André said this is the best place to find them."

"André also said there are three other entrances," Katie replied, "and they easily could have gone in one of those."

"I don't know…" Zack said slowly.

"I have an idea," Katie whispered, picking up the puppy and opening her oversized bag. Gently setting Butterball inside, the purse enveloped the puppy.

Zack's eyes got big. "We can't sneak her in like that!"

"We don't have a choice," Katie said. "It's either find her owners, or sacrifice this sweet puppy to that horrible uncle. He's no better than the pound."

Zack's eyebrows lowered. "But that's dishonest, Katie. You know André said dogs aren't allowed inside."

Katie picked up the bag and started toward the end of the line. "We'll get her in," she said over her shoulder.

As the line progressed slowly toward the entrance, Zack moved up beside Katie. A tiny *choo!* came from inside her bag.

"You can't get that close!" Katie said in a loud whisper, shoving him on ahead of her. "Just keep walking!"

"But I still don't—" he stopped short.

Instantly Katie realized why when her eyes landed on the X-ray machine sitting squarely in the entryway ahead. Every parcel, every bag rolled through the scanner. "Uh oh," she said softly, pulling her bag up against her.

Zack whirled around to face her and frantically motioned toward the X-ray machine.

Katie indicated for him to turn back around. "Keep going!" she whispered, clutching her bag tightly.

The young man right in front of Zack set his backpack on the conveyor belt and walked alongside the machine as his bag slid through the X-ray and out the other side. A female guard standing by the entrance door then motioned for Zack to step forward.

As he did, Katie watched the guard wrinkle her nose and take a step backward. She said something to Zack, but when he just looked at her with big eyes, she must have realized he didn't speak French. She turned to the man running the X-ray machine and said something that made him chuckle.

"It wasn't my fault!" Zack blurted out. "I don't wear perfume! I got sprayed!" he said, waving his arms in an attempt to demonstrate what had happened. The motion only circulated more of the strong scent throughout the pyramid enclosure.

The guard stepped around Zack and over to the X-ray machine, continuing to speak in French to the operator. Whatever she said got them both laughing, which led to a rapid conversation back and forth.

While all this was happening, Katie stealthily scooted past Zack, holding her bag close against her as she slipped on around to the escalator just beyond. Racing down the moving stairs, she came to a large central area with an info booth. Fanning out around it were guarded entrances into various sections of the Louvre.

Katie rapidly merged into the crowd in case someone was following her, then scooted around a corner not far from the escalator. Stopping to catch her breath, she reached in her bag and gave Butterball a congratulatory pat. "We made it, girl!" she said softly.

In a few moments, she heard Zack's voice nearby. "Katie!" he called in hoarse whisper, "where are you?"

She stuck her head around the corner. "Over here."

As Zack came toward her, she backed up a few steps, keeping some distance between them. Grinning at the boy she said, "Hey, your perfume sure paid off."

"Yeah, yeah, ha ha ha," he said, giving her a disgusted look. "Being laughed at so you could sneak in here wasn't my idea."

Katie's smile began to fade when she noticed a row of machines right behind Zack. A big sign overhead read *Tickets musée.*[52] "Oh no," she said, pointing. "Problem number two."

Just then a man walked up to one of the machines and slid a Euro bill into it. When he punched some buttons, a ticket popped out. Katie looked back at Zack and said, "I wonder how much it costs to get inside the museum."

---

52 Pronounced tee-kay myoo-zay, meaning museum tickets

To her surprise, the man turned toward her and said in perfect English, "The Louvre is free for anyone under eighteen." He looked them over quickly and smiled. "I think you qualify."

"Hey, that's great!" she said. "Thanks!"

The man stepped forward and handed her a folded paper. "Here's a map," he said. "Don't get lost." He then turned and disappeared into the throng.

When Zack moved up beside Katie and took the map, a sneeze came from inside her bag. Katie gave him a gentle shove. "You can't get that close, remember? Every time you do, Butterball sneezes, and it's going to give her away."

Zack stared into Katie's eyes. "Hey, it's not *my* fault." Glancing down at the bag he said, "She's not supposed to be in here anyway. Nothing ever makes lying and cheating okay."

"Well she's in here now…so you can't come close to us."

Setting his lips in a line, Zack stepped back without arguing further. Instead, he unfolded the map and quietly studied it for a while. Finally he said, "Wow, this place is huge."

"Great," Katie mumbled. "Where should we go?"

Zack turned the map at a different angle, looked around, then studied the map again. "Okay, there are four levels, and I think we're in the lowest one." He pointed toward an escalator. "If we go that way, the *Mona Lisa* is up two floors."

Katie shrugged. "So? Who's Mona Lisa?"

Zack's mouth dropped open. "You've never heard of Leonardo da Vinci and the *Mona Lisa*?"

Katie shook her head.

"It's like one of the most famous paintings in the world," he said. "Da Vinci was a guy who not only painted, but was also an inventor and an architect. He did all sorts of incredible stuff during the Renaissance." Zack paused, then added with a smile, "Homeschool."

"Okay. Well, we need to go where the people are," she said, starting in the direction he had pointed, "but don't get too close!"

As they walked toward the entrance to that section, Katie discovered she could hold her big bag up against her in a way that cradled Butterball and gave the puppy room to breathe, yet easily kept her concealed. So when they reached the first guard, she hugged her bag, smiled sweetly, and the man merely nodded as she went by.

Moving from one high-ceilinged room to another, Katie soon realized how right Zack had been—*This place is enormous!* Not only that, but as they passed by row after row of marble statues, she saw uniformed guards everywhere. *Fortunately, most of them look totally bored,* she noticed, scooting to the opposite side of the room from a watchman whose eyes kept drooping shut.

When they walked into yet another room of statues, Katie saw a crowd up ahead. Hurrying into the throng, she found everyone taking pictures of a marble lady with no arms named *Venus de Milo.* Katie looked every direction, but no family matched the description she needed. Working her way clear of the crowd she moved back near Zack, shook her head, and said, "Let's keep going."

Soon they entered a room of Egyptian artifacts and sphinxes. "Look at those," Zack said, pointing to a row of large carved monkeys with their arms up. He stood next to them and struck a pose.

Katie chuckled. "Yeah, you look the same...but the monkeys definitely smell better."

Zack laughed, then turned and looked into the next room. All at once his eyes lit up. "Mummies!" As he hurried past Katie toward the display of tombs and partially unwrapped bodies, she heard him say, "Amazing!"

Following him into the room, Katie wrinkled her nose and turned away to look out the window. *What's so amazing about a shriveled ol' dead person?* she wondered, starting toward the next section. "Come on," she called over her shoulder.

Leaving the Egyptians behind, they finally came to an area of the museum filled with paintings. By this time, Katie was starting to feel tired and grumpy. "My arms are killing me from carrying Butterball," she said, looking for someplace where she could discreetly set the bag down. "Are we anywhere near that moaning Lisa picture yet?"

"***Mona** Lisa*," Zack said, pulling out the map.

Spying an empty bench over by a window, Katie hurried toward it. She gently set Butterball and the bag on the floor and stretched her weary arms. "Ohhh, my muscles ache," she groaned, leaning back and resting her head against the windowsill. *It feels so good to close my eyes.*

But in the next instant, her eyelids flew open at the sound of Zack's urgent voice calling, "Butterball, no! Come back here!"

Chapter 15

Leaping up, Katie grabbed her bag, held on to her beret, and joined the chase. Up ahead she could see Butterball's little legs churning as the puppy dodged tourists right and left. Several people attempted to grab the fleeing animal, but somehow the puppy managed to twist and turn her pudgy body and slip past them all. "Butterball!" Katie yelled, but her voice had no effect whatsoever.

"Here, girl," Zack called from in front of Katie. But the puppy raced on.

As Katie followed Zack through a high archway into the next room, she saw a guard emerge from the shadows and try to nab the fleeing puppy. Butterball veered to her right just as the security official swung and caught empty air. On the puppy ran, skidding past people's legs, running underneath antique tables, weaving her way through priceless displays, and looking like she was having the time of her life.

Guards began to appear like ghosts out of the walls. Katie flew past an older watchman who looked like he hadn't walked that fast in years. "Butterball!" she cried out again, "come back here!" But the puppy slid on all fours around a corner and momentarily disappeared ahead of Zack into the next room.

When Katie reached the corner, she had to swerve to avoid a tangled pile of Zack's and several tourists' arms and legs. *If I don't get that puppy, there's going to be a bigger mess than that!* she thought, dodging a man who was starting to videotape the pileup.

By now, the noise had attracted quite a bit of attention, and people were either moving out of Butterball's way, or attempting to catch the puppy as she sped by. The museum's slick floor, however, made it difficult for people to keep their footing when they bent down to grab the scurrying animal.

Everywhere Katie looked, security personnel were talking loudly on their radios as they speed-walked after the fugitive. *I guess they've been told not to run,* she thought, *but they aren't going to catch her that way!*

Butterball's short legs sprinted as fast as they could go, carrying her past masterpiece paintings, ancient vases, and bronze busts of emperors from long ago.

But Katie was gaining ground.

They tore past a flight of stairs on their left, and from the corner of Katie's eye she saw the backs of three persons below—a tall, dark-haired man, a woman, and what she thought was a blonde girl in front of the adults. "Hey, wait a minute!" Katie yelled, but when they didn't even turn around, she hurried on.

Butterball finally seemed to be tiring. As she wiggled her body to the left, avoiding another guard, she lost her footing, sending her pudgy body tumbling like a rolling pin across the floor. "Gotcha!" Katie said, finally able to bend down and nab the miniature escape artist.

Gripping the puppy's collar tightly, Katie collapsed on the floor next to Butterball. The puppy's tongue hung practically to the floor, but she looked like she was laughing.

"You're a very naughty girl!" Katie scolded, pulling Butterball into her lap as she sat cross-legged on the hard museum floor.

Immediately a forest of dark blue legs surrounded her.

Looking up into a sea of cross faces, Katie swallowed hard as the realization hit her. *I'm going to be sent to French prison!*

Veronica Stewart put a hand up to her face as she studied the painting of Pontius Pilate washing his hands of Christ's blood. "What a horrible moment," she said to herself.

Just then she heard a long, drawn-out sigh behind her. She turned to see Lucy placing her hand over her mouth, covering an enormous yawn. "Tired, honey?" Mrs. Stewart asked, stepping over to put an arm around the girl's shoulders.

"Dead things and old pictures make me sleepy," she said, meeting her mother's eyes.

Mrs. Stewart smiled. "Okay, sweetie. We'll hurry through

here and—" She stopped and quickly turned toward the sound of agitated voices coming from down the hall.

"What's going on?" Russell Stewart said, swiveling around toward the room just behind them. Several security guards hurried past, one talking rapidly on his walkie talkie. Curious tourists also began moving toward the commotion.

Mr. Stewart grabbed Lucy's hand. "Come on," he said, abruptly turning to walk the other direction.

Mrs. Stewart followed. "What's happening?" she asked, not really expecting an answer.

"I don't know," her husband said over his shoulder, "but these days it's better not to stick around and find out." He directed them toward a stairway ahead and to the left.

Mrs. Stewart tried to move Lucy a little faster as the noise behind seemed to be getting closer. Hurrying down the stairs, they had almost reached the end of the first flight when Veronica Stewart heard someone say from above, "Hey, wait a minute!" But she didn't dare take the time to turn around.

After descending several flights of steps as swiftly as possible, they reached an exit out of the museum. But Russell Stewart didn't allow them to slow down until they had crossed the Pont des Arts bridge.

When they had arrived safely on the opposite side of the Seine, Mrs. Stewart leaned heavily against a stone building. "Gracious!" she panted, trying to catch her breath. Looking down at her daughter she said, "Are you okay, Luce?"

The girl turned a serious face up to her mother. "I'm fine, Mommy. But what were we running from?"

Mr. Stewart put a hand on his daughter's head. "I don't know, Lucy. There was some sort of trouble inside the museum, and in these times it's just better to avoid public places when something doesn't seem right." He paused. "I'm sure everything is fine...but we wanted to be sure."

"Actually," Veronica Stewart said with a twinkle in her eye, "you told us you were getting tired, so we just hurried to get you out."

"Mom..." Lucy giggled.

Mrs. Stewart smiled. "Anyhow, I'll bet you wouldn't mind having dinner, huh?"

"Yes!" Lucy said, taking her mother's hand.

"And," Mr. Stewart added, "we need to pack up and get ready to take Big Blue down to Marseille in the morning."

Lucy's smile faded as she turned to look up at her father. "Once we leave Paris," she said softly, "I'll never be able to find Butterball again."

Veronica Stewart squeezed her daughter's hand, feeling a weight in her heart for them both.

"*Comment vas-tu?*" one of the guards said.

Katie started to stand, holding Butterball tightly in her arms. "I don't understand," she shook her head.

"Oh. You are okay?" one of the male guards asked in a heavy French accent.

"I'm fine," Katie said. She glanced around at the grim faces. "But...am I going to jail?"

"Come with me," another guard said, motioning for the cluster to let Katie through.

As the other watchmen scattered back to their posts, the tall, harsh-looking guard clamped a firm hand on her shoulder and guided her toward a seat by an open window. Katie felt like she was being placed in an execution chair.

While she sat on the hard wooden bench, the guard stood in front of her with folded arms, glaring at her like she was a hardened criminal. Katie didn't know what to say, so she stroked Butterball and waited for her sentencing.

Soon Zack raced around the corner, his hair sticking out in every direction. *Boy, am I glad to see you!* Katie thought, giving him a weak smile as he came up beside the sentry. The stern official wiggled his nose a little as he glanced toward the boy, but even that couldn't bring a real smile to Katie's face.

"Is Butterball okay?" Zack asked, standing a few feet to the guard's side.

Katie nodded. "She's fine, but…I think they're going to put me in prison."

Zack turned to the guard. "What happens now?" he asked.

"The security chief is coming," he said curtly, not taking his eyes from Katie.

She swallowed hard and looked down at the puppy. *I'm going to be stuck in jail and Butterball is going to end up with the Monster Uncle after all,* she thought, blinking hard to hold back tears. *I've totally messed up everything.*

Another dark-suited guard arrived shortly. *He must be the chief,* she thought as the two watchmen spoke for a few moments.

When the new guard sat down next to her, the first sentry turned to leave. She faced this official and found his eyes to be far kinder.

"*Bonjour*," he said. "I am head of security."

Katie gave a slight nod, but Butterball began to wag enthusiastically. *She'd be happy to meet Darth Vader*, Katie thought, keeping her eyes on the man.

The chief placed a gentle hand on the puppy's back and said, "Dogs are not allowed inside the Louvre, Mademoiselle. You can see why."

Katie nodded. "Do we…" she gulped, "do we have to go to jail?"

The corners of the security chief's mouth rose ever so slightly. "Prison? No, no, of course not, *cheri*." His face became serious again. "But I must warn you about doing this kind of thing again." With that he gave her a brief scolding which ended with, "and you must take the dog outside right now."

Katie nodded. "I'm sorry," she said softly. "We were just desperate to find the puppy's owners and I thought they were in here."

As the guard stood up, he said, "You are welcome back into the Louvre—but the dog *must* stay outside."

The security chief escorted them down the same stairwell where Katie thought she had seen the American family. After leading them outside and giving them another warning, he turned and disappeared back into the museum. Zack immediately faced her and said, "See, I *told* you we shouldn't take her inside." He shook his head and added almost to himself, "Being dishonest never works out."

At hearing his words, Katie felt her heart drop. *Yep, I blew it again. But I can't think about that right now.* "Yeah, okay," she said quickly, "but Zack, I saw a family just like we've been looking for! They were running down the stairs when I was chasing Butterball."

Zack shrugged. "Well they're long gone by now."

Katie stood on tiptoes and looked all around, but Zack was right; they were nowhere in sight. As she dropped back to her feet, the realization hit her like a Mac truck—"The Louvre was our last shot," she said softly, "because now we can't even offer her to anyone else."

Kneeling down, Katie stroked the puppy's head. Butterball placed her front paws on the girl's knees and seemed to grin from ear to ear. Katie blinked back tears. *Sweet puppy, if you knew what was going to happen tomorrow morning, you wouldn't be smiling.* Katie almost felt sick with worry. *So what can we do now?*

CHAPTER 16

Katie and Zack slowly and silently headed home with Butterball trotting happily beside them. Katie felt like she was dragging her heart along on the leash, rather than a carefree puppy.

When they arrived at the house, the Boulangers were just sitting down for dinner. The moment Zack stepped into the dining room, Monsieur Boulanger's head shot up. He looked at the boy and frowned slightly. Katie saw Zack's face grow as red as the bright tablecloth in front of them. "I'm going to take a shower," he mumbled, swiveling 180 degrees and hurrying up the stairs.

"I see you did not find the puppy's family," Madame Boulanger said, looking down at Butterball.

"No, ma'am," Katie replied softly. She didn't have the heart to mention the events at the Louvre. Instead, she met the kind woman's eyes and said, "I think I'll just feed Butterball, take her out, and then go to bed…if that's okay."

"No dinner?" Madame asked, her eyes widening.

Katie shook her head and turned around to take Butterball back downstairs for her puppy chow.

All that night, Katie tossed and turned with terrible dreams about evil giants trying to eat the puppy. When a knock on the door startled her awake the next morning, she didn't feel too great.

"Katie?" came André's voice through a crack.

"Yes?" She struggled to rise up on an elbow. Butterball scooted her warm body closer against the girl.

"Time to get up," he said. "We leave for Uncle Pierre's in an hour."

"O…kay," she answered slowly, panic rising at his words.

Katie gently pushed Butterball a little ways across the bed. "Sweet girl," Katie said, "I'd gladly give you the *whole* bed every night, if you could just stay here."

After showering and getting dressed, Katie stood in front of the mirror in her room, looking at her reflection. *I'd do almost anything to save that precious puppy from both Uncle Pierre and the pound,* she thought with a sigh. *One's as bad as the other!*

Then her eyes fell on the Bible study booklet André had given her. It had dropped open on the dresser to one of the dog-eared pages.

Read:

"*Who may climb the mountain of the Lord? Who may stand in his holy place? Only those whose hands and hearts are pure, who do not worship idols and never tell lies. They will receive the Lord's blessing and have right standing with God their savior*" (Psalm 24:3-5).

Learn:

David, a wonderful king of Israel, wrote Psalm 24, and God called David "a man after His own heart." Wow, what an incredible thing for God to call someone! Was it because David was perfect? No, only Jesus Christ lived a perfect life on earth. But David had a passionate desire to serve and please God in all that he said and did, and he was quick to confess his sins. David reminds us that in order to receive blessings from God, we need to have pure hearts and hands.

Apply:

In those verses, God gives us two specific areas to check—idols and lies. An idol is anything in your life more important to you than Jesus, and a lie is anything that is not true, no matter how small. Is there anything taking the place of Jesus in your life? Is there anything you have lied about that hasn't been confessed to God *and* to the person you said it to? If either of these is true of you, confess that to God right now, and then confess any lies to the person(s) who heard them. You can have a heart and hands that are pure, and be in right standing before God!

I don't totally understand all this... but I sure recognize the heaviness in my heart, she thought as she walked slowly over to the bed. *Mrs. Cassidy called it 'conviction.'*

Katie sat down, closed her eyes, and took a deep breath. "I'm sorry I did it again, God," she started. "I really do want to have a pure heart and hands, and I'm very sorry about sneaking Butterball into the Louvre…really. Please help me stop doing stuff like that."

Right then Butterball made a snorting sound, and Katie looked over at the puppy sleeping in her box. "But God," she added, "please don't punish Butterball because I've messed up. Please keep her from going to Uncle Pierre's or the pound. Please, God, help us find another way." She stopped for a moment, then added, "That's as honest as I know how to be, God. I really want to do better…but right now, please help this poor puppy."

When Katie stood up again, she noticed that even though she was still very concerned about Butterball, the discouragement that had been weighing on her since last night now seemed less. *That's sort of amazing,* she thought as she picked up the study pamphlet. *I really need to do this every day.* Folding the paper booklet in two, she stuck it in the back pocket of her shorts, then bent down and hooked the leash on Butterball's collar.

When Katie arrived in the dining room for breakfast, she was surprised to find the entire family there. She looked at Madame with puzzled eyes. "On Fridays the bakery is closed," the lady said, "so we will spend a few hours in the country…at Pierre's."

Katie just nodded and sat down. Simply hearing that name started to bring the knot back to her stomach and erase the peace she had just felt. She met André's gentle brown eyes, and he looked like he understood what was going on inside her. She wanted to plead with him for another option—*anything!*—but she couldn't think of how to do that with Monsieur Boulanger sitting there across from her.

Forcing down a few bites of croissant, Katie soon excused herself to finish getting ready. She took Butterball to her room, shut the door, and burst into tears. Dropping to her knees by the bed, she grabbed a pillow and put it over her head so the family wouldn't hear.

Soon a knock sounded on her door. "Yes?" she answered weakly, looking up from under the pillow.

"Katie?" came Zack's voice.

"What?"

"We're going now."

Off to the torture chamber, she thought, getting up slowly while trying to dry her eyes. Seeing her beret hanging from the corner of the mirror, she settled it on her head, hoping it would take attention away from her puffy face. Then she picked up the puppy and carried her down to the car.

Monsieur and Madame Boulanger sat in the two front seats, while Katie squeezed in the middle of the small car's backseat between the boys. Thankfully Zack seemed to have scrubbed his perfume down to a faint whiff.

Katie stroked Butterball's soft fur as they wove their way through the streets of Paris and out into the countryside. Once she glanced at Zack on her left, and he tried to give her a little smile. But Katie could see her own sadness mirrored in his eyes.

In fact, she noticed that the entire car felt like a tomb on wheels. Katie looked over at André and found his head bowed and his eyes closed. *How can he sleep at a time like this?!*

Just then the boy looked up. Leaning forward toward his father, André said, "Papa?"

"Mmmm?" Monsieur Boulanger leaned his head a little toward his son so he could hear, while keeping his eyes on the road.

Katie didn't understand a word of the conversation that ensued, but she watched André's face transform from intense to what looked like hopeful. She could also see a little of Monsieur Boulanger's reactions, and he first seemed surprised, then maybe a little angry. But as he listened to his son, his face softened.

When André stopped talking, there was a moment of dead silence. Then Monsieur Boulanger said something that seemed to catch his son off guard. The teenager broke into a smile, let out a long breath, and sat back in the seat, beaming.

Katie turned questioning eyes to him. André looked at her and said, "Papa told me I can audition for music school, and after he hears their evaluation, we will talk further. It is a very encouraging step."

"Really?" Katie and Zack said together.

André nodded, still radiant.

"Wow," Zack said. "That's great, André."

"Yeah, André, that's good news," Katie said, trying to sound cheerful. But her heart still felt like a lead weight in her chest.

André and his parents began talking back and forth, and Katie assumed it was about his new direction in life. But for her, the car ride still felt like The Drive of Doom.

Katie and Zack spoke very little for the next half hour… until Butterball suddenly stood up on Katie's lap and started to make a circle.

"Uh oh," Katie said.

André stopped whatever he was saying to his parents and turned toward her. "What is wrong?"

"Butterball needs to go," Katie said. "She always does this sort of circling thing when she's about to wee. Actually…I need to go too," she added softly.

Madame Boulanger said something to her husband and began to motion toward a service station up ahead. "*Là! Là!*" she pointed urgently.

I sure hope we make it! Katie thought, trying to distract the puppy while they turned off the two-lane highway into the filling station. *This could get really yucky!*

"Hey, look," Zack said as they pulled past a large blue SUV parked in front of the station. "You don't see those big ol' things over here. And it's got an American license plate!"

Katie couldn't have cared less. The instant the car came to a stop, she pushed against Zack, practically shoving him out the door. She then leaped out and rushed Butterball over toward a patch of grass at the side of the parking lot. The puppy squatted and released a torrent.

"Man alive!" Katie said. "I'm sure glad you didn't do that on *me!*"

Zack had gotten back in the car, so the minute Butterball finished, Katie quickly set the puppy on his lap and sprinted toward the bathroom inside the station. Finding a door with a picture of a lady in a skirt, she twisted the handle, but it was locked.

"Ohhhh," Katie moaned, starting to hop up and down a little.

"Be right there!" a woman called from inside.

Soon the door opened, and Katie barely glanced at the pretty blue-eyed woman who held the door and said, "There you go."

"Thanks!" Katie rushed past her and locked the bolt.

When she got back to the car and opened the door, Zack set Butterball on the seat and climbed out so Katie could scoot into the middle again. "You're so nice," she muttered sarcastically, poking him in the ribs.

"Don't mention it," he grinned slightly.

"Ready?" Monsieur Boulanger asked, sounding annoyed.

"Uh huh, thanks," Katie said.

Their car backed out of the parking lot, turned onto the highway, and resumed their route south. *On toward the monster's house,* Katie sighed, leaning back in the seat and reaching up to straighten her hair. *My beret!*

After a second of frantically looking around, Katie yelled, "Wait a minute!" so loud that Monsieur jerked the wheel slightly.

He grumbled something that she didn't want translated.

"I left my beret in the bathroom!" she said. "I *really* don't want to lose it."

Monsieur Boulanger did *not* look happy, but his wife

obviously said something that meant "go back," because he pulled off at the next exit and circled around, retracing their path to the filling station.

As they pulled into the parking lot again, Monsieur wheeled around the big SUV that was just starting to back up. The moment he brought their car to a stop, Katie pushed against Zack. "Hold your horses, for Pete's sake!" he said, unbuckling his seatbelt and opening the door.

After he got out, Butterball tumbled out, followed by Katie. She handed the leash to Zack and started around the car toward the station, when she heard a funny pounding sound. It didn't really register where it was coming from—until the skidding of tires on the pavement nearby made her turn to see the blue SUV sliding to a halt. In the back window was a little blonde girl pounding on the glass with one hand and waving wildly with the other.

Katie froze. *No way!* she thought, watching the SUV back slowly into a parking spot near the Boulangers. The instant the large vehicle came to a stop, the side door flew open and a young girl leaped out.

"Butterball!" the girl yelled, hurrying toward them.

It took Katie a second to grasp that this girl knew the puppy's name. Then Katie's mouth dropped open. "Yes!" She started to smile. "Yes, this is Butterball!"

The girl collapsed on the pavement beside the puppy, hugging and kissing the happy animal. Butterball wagged furiously, then crawled up into the girl's lap and began licking her face.

"Oh my goodness!" a woman said, hurrying around from

the passenger side. "I can't believe this! It's really Butterball?"

Katie nodded, feeling a lump—a *good* lump—forming in her throat. "We've been looking all over Paris for you," Katie said, her voice cracking. "We've been everywhere!"

"This is a miracle," the woman said, putting her hands to her face.

By now the Boulangers and the little girl's father had joined the group, and everyone started talking at once. Katie couldn't stop smiling as she watched the girl cradle Butterball, rocking back and forth saying, "We found you! We found you!"

Madame Boulanger stepped over next to Katie and put an arm around the girl. "*Très bien*, Katie," she said. "I am *so* happy the puppy has found its owners." She bent near the girl's ear and whispered, "I did not want her to go to the pound *or* to Pierre's!"

Katie wiped tears from her eyes and leaned against the sweet woman, savoring this special moment.

The little girl's father introduced his family, then Madame Boulanger said, "And allow me to introduce our group. These are our friends, Katie and Zack, and my son, André," she motioned toward each one. "And this is my husband, Jacques Boulanger, and I am Monique Brineaux Boulanger."

Mrs. Stewart's eyes widened, and she quickly asked, "Did you say your name was Monique Brineaux…spelled B-r-i-n-e-a-u-x?"

Madame nodded with a puzzled expression. "*Oui*, it is my maiden name. It is rather unusual, but I like it, so I keep it as part of my name."

A look of amazement covered Mrs. Stewart's face. "Yes, it is very unusual. In fact, Brineaux is also *my* maiden name. My grandfather and his brother had to flee during World War II, and my grandfather—one of those brothers—escaped to America."

"No!" Madame's jaw dropped. She hesitated a moment, then slowly asked, "Was your grandfather's name Edgard Brineaux?"

CHAPTER 17

Katie thought Mrs. Stewart might faint! She clutched her chest, and her face turned white as she whispered, "Yes, Grandfather's name was Edgard Brineaux—which means *you* are my lost relative!"

The two women immediately began talking at the same time, launching into a conversation that didn't seem to include breathing. Katie shook her head in amazement and turned away to sit cross-legged on the pavement in front of Lucy and Butterball. Zack plopped down beside them.

Seeing Lucy's shining blue eyes, Katie couldn't help but grin. "Boy, am I glad we found you," Katie said.

"Me too! Oh, me too!" the girl replied, continuing to rock back and forth as she hugged the puppy.

Katie glanced at Zack and noticed that he looked just as

happy. *It feels like we've been through our own World War—which suddenly turned into one big party.*

Butterball slapped her tail back and forth as she turned to look at Katie, and all at once Katie realized this would be her last moments with the puppy.

"She likes you," Lucy said.

"I like her a lot too." Katie reached out to stroke Butterball's soft fur.

Lucy met Katie's eyes. "Thanks for taking good care of her. And this red scarf around her neck is cute."

"Oh, my beret!" Katie said, remembering the hat that matched Butterball's scarf. "Be right back."

When Katie emerged from the building, beret in hand, her heart overflowed as she watched the various little groups talking in the parking lot. The two husbands and André all stood with arms folded, looking like businessmen at a meeting; Madame Boulanger and Mrs. Stewart were holding hands and chattering non-stop, their faces close together; and Zack and Lucy both sat patting the special puppy that had brought them all together. *This is **perfect**,* she thought with a contented sigh.

Just then Katie heard Mrs. Stewart say, "Can we all go for coffee?"

"*Oui!*" Madame replied quickly. She stepped over to her husband, and after a brief conversation, he made a call on his cell phone.

Soon Monsieur announced in his halting English, "I tell my brother, 'We no bring dog, we find owners. Now we go for quick café, then we go to his house for short visit.'"

"Yay!" Katie sang out.

"Wonderful!" Veronica Stewart said, clasping her hands together as she turned toward her husband. "Monique and I have a lifetime to catch up on."

Mr. Stewart smiled. "Honey, you also have a lifetime left to build memories, so it doesn't *all* have to happen in the next hour."

They piled back in their cars, and Monsieur Boulanger led them into a nearby town. As they took seats around an outside table at a charming café, André put a hand on Zack's shoulder. "I think you had better stick with *chocolat chaud,*[53] *mon ami*," he said.

"What's that?" Zack asked.

"Hot chocolate."

Katie, Zack, and André all laughed.

The next hour flew by as everyone learned more about one another. Then all too soon, the Stewarts and the Boulangers began exchanging contact information with promises to meet again very soon. Katie overheard Mrs. Stewart say to Madame Boulanger, "I'll call you tomorrow morning."

When the party gathered one last time in the parking lot to give final farewells, Katie walked over toward Lucy, who was holding Butterball's leash. When the puppy saw Katie, she let out a "yip!" and took a bounce toward the girl.

Katie bent down and lifted the puppy up in front of her one last time. Looking into those gentle black eyes, a lump rose again in Katie's throat as she said softly, "You be good, okay? No wetting

---

53 Pronounced show-koe-lah showed

in flower beds or running through museums, you hear?"

Butterball's tail flew back and forth through the air.

Katie kissed the puppy's nose and set her back down beside Lucy. "Take good care of her, okay?" Katie said softly, giving the little girl a hug.

"I will!" Lucy threw her arms tightly around the girl. "Thank you for saving Butterball."

Katie swallowed hard.

Lucy led the puppy toward the SUV, then turned around and waved, "Bye, Katie! Bye, Zack!"

They both waved back.

Katie watched as the girl hoisted Butterball into the vehicle, then climbed in behind. As the SUV slowly pulled away, Katie could see the back of Lucy's head through the rear window… when all of a sudden Butterball appeared. The puppy dropped her head on Lucy's shoulder and looked out the back window at Katie.

Raising her hand slightly, Katie whispered, "Bye, Butterball," her voice breaking.

Once the SUV had disappeared, Katie and Zack piled back into the Boulangers' car and headed to Uncle Pierre's. Fortunately, the time there went by quickly. Over lunch, the two kids talked to one another while the adults carried on their own conversation in French. Then during the car ride home, Katie continually grinned as she listened to everyone chattering, often at the same time. *You'd never know this was the same car as the one coming down!*

When they neared Paris, Katie glanced out the window and

saw the Eiffel Tower. A flood of memories from the past four days crossed her mind, making her smile. *Thanks, God, for this amazing adventure—and for how You worked everything out. You answered my prayers in an* ***awesome*** *way!*

When they arrived home, André bolted out of the car and hurried on ahead of them, meeting them on the first floor with his accordion. "It is a day to celebrate!" he said, leading them into the living room where he quickly launched into an upbeat French musette, followed by a jazz piece. The moment he finished, his audience burst into applause.

When the clapping stopped, Monsieur Boulanger cleared his throat in a way that drew everyone's attention. "I say in English," he glanced at Katie and Zack, then back to his son. "André, I not know you play so well. I am…."

"Impressed!" his wife filled in for him.

The man nodded. "Yes. Very impressed. You have talent you must use." He smiled with a gentleness that Katie hadn't seen before.

André dropped his head a little. "*Merci*, Papa," he said softly. "*Merci*."

After a few more minutes of music, they all adjourned to the dining room for a delightful strawberry tart. When Katie had finished the last crumbs off her plate, she looked around at this family who had welcomed her in and said, "Thank you all so much…for *everything*. We've both had an incredible time." She glanced at Zack with a grin. "Especially at the perfume shop."

Zack smiled and said, "Yeah, but *especially* on the balcony of Notre Dame."

She started to giggle. "No, I think the canal at Versailles was the best."

"No, definitely the mopeds by the Eiffel Tower!" Zack said, and they both burst out laughing, leaving Madame and Monsieur with puzzled expressions.

"Well," Madame Boulanger said with a shrug, "you are both most welcome."

Katie composed herself and said, "I guess we'll be heading home this afternoon, since Émilie is coming back, and Butterball's gone, and all."

Madame smiled. "We have enjoyed you so much. I hope you will come back."

"And," André reached into his pocket, "how about one last ice cream for you two? My gift."

"Great!" Katie said, rising to her feet and spontaneously going over to give Madame Boulanger a hug.

The woman stood and kissed both of Katie's cheeks, saying, "Thank you for adding so much joy to our home."

Katie turned around, expecting to find André. But instead, she almost bumped into Monsieur Boulanger's towering body. He looked down at her with an expression not of sternness, but rather of amusement. "*Oui*, Katie. We enjoy you much. You are"—he searched for the word—"lively."

Katie giggled. "*My* father calls it 'hyper,'" she said.

He took her hand and gave it a gentle squeeze. When their eyes met, she was surprised at the warmth and kindness she saw there.

Then Katie turned and gave André a big hug. "Thanks, André," she said, and he also kissed her cheeks, making her blush.

"Okie dokie," Zack said over by the stairs, shifting from one foot to the other. "Thanks again, everybody!" He gave a slight wave, then turned toward the steps.

Katie and Zack raced down the stairwell and into the courtyard outside. As they turned into the passageway toward the street, Katie felt like her heart was singing. "Mr. Gateman sure gave us—" She stopped dead in her tracks. Just ahead, almost filling the entire opening to the street, stood an enormous man. "It's you!" Katie yelled, running straight toward the figure and barreling into his powerful body.

Mr. Gateman laughed with the deep, resonate sound she loved so much. "Well, it's good to see you too, Katie. And you as well, Zack."

"Hello, sir," Zack said, stopping in front of the man.

Mr. Gateman took Katie's arms and pulled her back a little so he could look in her face. "And how have you enjoyed Paris?"

"It's been amazing!" she said, then hesitated. "It's an incredible place…but I would have had even more fun if I hadn't been so worried about Butterball."

He smiled. "Katie, life is always a combination of joys and challenges. That is why spending time in God's Word each day is so important—so you will know *how* to meet those challenges."

"Yeah, you know what?" Katie replied with a grin. "Each time I read the Bible verses in that book André gave me, I wasn't so worried or grumpy anymore."

Zack scooted back a step and said, "You should *definitely* read that every day."

Katie ignored him, because in that instant, a lightbulb went on inside her head. "I understand your note!" she said in amazement. "When you wrote that I was supposed to learn something about my relationship with my Father that would transform me, you weren't talking about *my* Dad, were you? It was about my relationship with my *heavenly* Father, and how He transforms me when I read His Word, right?"

Mr. Gateman chuckled. "Katie, you always bring me joy." He put a hand on her shoulder. "Yes, I want you to understand how important it is that you help your new spiritual nature grow to be more like Jesus by feeding it from the Word of God. And," he paused for a moment, "there was another part to my note, remember?" Mr. Gateman's eyes met hers, and she had that familiar sense he could read her mind. "What have you learned about yourself, Katie?"

She dropped her head. *I might as well tell the truth, 'cause that's what this is all about.* Softly she said, "I…I haven't been very honest lately."

Mr. Gateman put his finger under her chin and brought her face up to look at him again. "I'm glad you recognize that, Katie. Keep practicing what you have learned, and you will be amazed at the results."

"Yes, sir," she said.

He smiled at her again. "And now, there are just a few loose ends."

She frowned. "Loose ends? You mean there's *more* I'm supposed to learn here?"

He looked beyond her toward Zack as he said, "You will

know, Katie. I trust that you will know." He paused, stepped back, and motioned for them to walk on out to the sidewalk. "But right now, it's time for Berthillon's."

"Yes!" Zack said, nudging Katie forward.

Passing Mr. Gateman, Katie started to turn around and ask, "Can you come with—?" But he was gone. She shook her head. *Every time!*

Zack looked back. "He did it again, huh?"

Katie nodded. "Sort of his signature thing, I guess," she said with a shrug and a smile.

"I wanted to tell him how much fun *I've* had in Paris," Zack said, walking on toward Berthillon's. "You know, even with trying to find Butterball's family, we've had a great time, huh, Katie?" He looked at her and added, "I mean, hey, you got to ride a horse around the palace of Versailles!"

Instantly Katie felt that familiar sense of conviction. "Yeah," she said softly as she stopped walking. "Hey, Zack?"

"Huh?" He turned toward her. "What'd I say?"

"About me riding English...um...I need to tell you something." She took a deep breath, then honestly described how she'd been given special abilities to not only ride English, but to scuba dive, to rope, and—she gulped hard—even how to ride Tango at his ranch.

Zack's eyes got wider and wider as she talked, and his jaw almost dropped to the ground. When she finished her explanation, Zack ran a hand through his wavy red hair and said, "Holy smokes! That's incredible! You mean, you couldn't even *ride a horse?*"

Katie stared at the pavement. She had a sinking feeling that now Zack wasn't going to like her as much, or he'd think she was just some dumb girl.

Feeling a light punch on her arm, she looked up to see him smiling. "But hey," he said, "you sure can ride now!" He paused. "You just can't play the accordion."

That made her laugh. And suddenly she realized how once again she felt the wonderful lightness that always came from doing the right thing. *I'll bet that was a loose end Mr. Gateman just talked about!*

Continuing on to Berthillon's, she and Zack chattered away about all the incredible things they'd gotten to do in this fascinating city. And in no time at all, they had licked up every last drop of their cones and were headed back to the Boulangers'.

Upon reaching the bakery, Katie pulled open the back door and stepped in—but the entire place was pitch black.

CHAPTER 18

Except for the small slivers of moonlight creeping through the curtains, Katie couldn't see much in the darkness at first. But it wasn't just the dim light. She instantly realized, *I'm back home in my bedroom!* It always took her a moment to adjust after being transported.

She looked down, and sure enough, she was back in her nightgown—except she still wore her shorts underneath. Giggling softly, she thought, *Mr. Gateman goofed on that one.* But when she felt something stiff in the back pocket, she remembered André's Bible study. ***That's** why I've still got my shorts on!* Then she reached up and felt her head. No beret. *Bummer! I didn't get to bring it back.*

As she started to pull her shorts off, she thought about how her favorite paperback book had served its purpose in getting her to Cassidy Ranch, and then had disappeared. *So I guess the beret must have served its purpose in bringing us together with the Stewarts at the gas station, and now it's gone.* She smiled. *But the Bible study has **lots** more purpose!*

Hearing footsteps coming down the hall, Katie sprang into bed and pulled the sheets up just as her mother's head poked through the door. "Katie?"

"Hi Mom," she said, trying not to sound wide awake.

"I heard you making some noise in here. You're still not asleep?"

Immediately Katie remembered how her mother had caught her reading right before she had been taken to Paris…and that she hadn't been honest with her Mom. *Another loose end!*

"Mom?"

"Yes?" Mrs. Carlson came over and stood beside Katie's bed.

"You know when you asked me if I'd been reading under the covers, and I told you 'no'?"

Her mother waited.

"Well…I was reading. I heard you coming, and I turned the flashlight off." Katie paused. "I'm sorry, Mom. I shouldn't have told you that."

Deborah Carlson sat down on the edge of the bed next to Katie and laid a loving hand on her daughter's shoulder. "Thank you, sweetheart, for telling me the truth."

The light from the open door illuminated her mother's face, and Katie could see the tenderness in her eyes.

"Honey," her mother continued, "it's always important to be honest, even when it hurts…so thank you."

Katie scooted out of the covers a little, sat up, and wrapped her arms around her mother, giving her a big squeeze. "Love you, Mom."

"Oh, Katie, I love you too." Her mom gave her a tight hug, then pulled back a little and looked into her daughter's hazel eyes. "You are turning into such an amazing young lady this summer!"

It's been an amazing summer! Katie thought, smiling as images of Cassidy Ranch, Hope Town, and now Paris flashed through her mind.

Mrs. Carlson rose to go, but when she reached Katie's door, she turned around slowly. "Katie, I know you've been sort of restless lately. Maybe we need to find you a hobby. What do you think?"

"Really?" Katie sat up farther in the bed. "Can I learn to play the accordion?"

"What?" Mrs. Carlson asked, clearly caught off guard.

"It's an incredible instrument, Mom. It's like an entire mobile orchestra, with all these sounds and keys and buttons and stuff," Katie said. "And you can play awesome jazz."

Mrs. Carlson chuckled. "Okay, honey, we'll look into it." She shook her head slightly. "You're just full of surprises this summer."

Katie couldn't help but grin.

"Good night, sweetie." Her mom shut the door behind her.

Dropping back on the pillow, Katie put an arm under her head and looked at the ceiling. "I think that's all the loose ends, huh, God?" she said softly. "Thanks for all You're teaching me. And...I can hardly wait to see what's going to happen next!"

Before you close this book: ☺

Katie found out how important it is to be truthful—in *every* situation. God tells us in the Bible, "*Truth stands the test of time; lies are soon exposed*" (Proverbs 12:19). Katie also discovered that dishonesty is very displeasing to God, and she told God she wants to live in a way that pleases Him.

Is there anything in your life about which you haven't been completely honest? God tells us, "*If we confess our sins to him, he is faithful and just to forgive us and to cleanse us from every wrong*" (1 John 1:9). You can confess any dishonesty right now and experience the same joy that Katie experiences when she does the right thing. Here is a prayer you can pray:

> Dear God, I confess that I have not been totally honest. Please forgive me for saying (fill in whatever you've said). Please give me Your strength to guard my tongue and watch what I say so that I can live in a way that pleases You. Thank You so much for your forgiveness. In Jesus' name, Amen.

Katie also discovered that when she spent time reading God's Word, it "fed" her new nature, changed her attitude, and opened her eyes to God's truths. God tells us in Romans 12:2: "*Don't copy the behavior and customs of this world, but let God transform you into a new person by changing the way you think. Then you will know what God wants you to do, and you will know how good and pleasing and perfect his will really is.*"

And guess what! You can read ***30 Days with God***—the daily Bible book André gave Katie and Zack—right along with them! In ***30 Days with God,*** you'll discover questions Zack and Katie have, things they are learning, and how it affects their lives. Don't miss out on a single moment of Katie's and Zack's adventures!

30 Days with God can be downloaded for free or purchased at www.KatieandZackAdventures.com.
Also available for purchase at www.Amazon.com.

Blessings as you continue in this wonderful journey of knowing and growing more like Christ!

Judy Starr, Katie Carlson, and Zack Cassidy

For Thought and Discussion

Chapter 1

1. Katie and Zack are transported to the beautiful city of Paris, France! Find Paris on a world map or globe. Then look at how far away it is from Oklahoma and Colorado, Katie's and Zack's homes.

2. While Katie is following André toward his family's store, she recalls telling her mother that she'd been trying to sleep, when she had really been reading under the covers. Do you think that was okay? Why?

Chapter 2

1. When Katie gets a note from Mr. Gateman, she doesn't know what her big job is, or what she's supposed to learn about herself or her relationship with her Father. What would you guess Mr. Gateman means?

2. Zack and Katie really want to find Butterball's owners, especially after learning that the puppy must go to the pound in five days. If you were in their situation, how would you feel?

Chapter 3

1. Why did the French people revolt during the time of Louis the Sixteenth and kill the King and Queen? Do you think the people did the right thing? Why?

2. What important lesson did Katie learn in the Bahamas that she now has to practice again with Zack? Give an example of how you have practiced this lately.

Chapter 4

1. The Stewart family has just moved to France for Mr. Stewart's new job. But both Lucy and Mrs. Stewart are struggling. What is difficult for them? If you have ever experienced a move to a new place, describe how you felt.

2. Katie is fascinated with the amazing sounds of the accordion. Would you like to play a musical instrument? Which one?

Chapter 5

1. Before coming to Paris, Katie told her mom she wasn't reading under the covers. Then in Paris she told André that Butterball knocked her into the Seine River, and now she told him she can play piano really well. Why do you think Katie is saying these things?

2. While looking around inside the Notre Dame cathedral, Zack sees a long row of wood carvings depicting Christ's appearances after He rose from the grave. The Bible tells us, *"Christ died for our sins, just as the Scriptures said. He was buried, and he was raised from the dead on the third day, as the Scriptures said. He was seen by Peter and then by the twelve apostles. After that, he was seen by more than five hundred of his followers"* (1 Corinthians 15:3-6). Why do you think the resurrection is so important to our faith in Jesus?

Chapter 6

1. Stuck on the Notre Dame balcony beside ugly gargoyles, Katie confesses her dishonesty to God and asks for His help. Does He answer her prayer? What happens?

2. André told Katie, "When we receive Christ's forgiveness, the Bible says we are given a new nature inside us." And with Christ's new nature living inside us, we want to do and say things more like Him. In 1 Peter 2:24 we read, "*He personally carried away our sins in his own body on the cross so we can be dead to sin and live for what is right.*" If you've never received Christ's forgiveness for your sins and asked Him to come into your life, you can pray the simple prayer Katie prayed at Cassidy Ranch right now:

> "Dear Jesus, I do believe in You, and I thank You for Your offer to pay the penalty for all my sins and mistakes. I know I do lots of stuff I shouldn't, so I receive Your payment for all those things. And I ask You to come into my life so I can be with You forever."

If you just prayed that prayer, you'll want to tell someone. Now you can start to "feed that new nature" like Katie is learning to do.

Chapter 7

1. What honor did the Eiffel Tower have when it was built in 1899 that it held for over thirty years (until the Empire State Building was built in New York City in 1931)?

2. When Katie started to say she hadn't cut in line at the Eiffel Tower, and Zack confronted her about it, she thought it wasn't a big deal. Do you think her dishonesty is "a big deal?" Why?

Chapter 8

1. While searching for a horse and buggy, Zack and Katie take a terrifying ride around Paris on the back of two mopeds. Have you ever been in a situation where you were really afraid? What did you do?

2. Katie is starting to become quite anxious about not finding Butterball's owners and about the looming possibility of the puppy going to the pound. What does she learn about Uncle Pierre and the people at the bakery? Do you have any other ideas for her?

Chapter 9

1. Zack and Katie got off the metro beside what looks like the Statue of Liberty. What are some things that are different in a foreign country that could make it challenging to get around?
2. Katie is so excited about getting to ride a horse around the palace of Versailles! But before she mounts, she discovers that the horses are trained to ride English—and she only knows how to ride Western! What would you do if you were in her place?

Chapter 10

1. Mrs. Stewart is trying to find information about her grandfather who helped hide Jews during World War II. Why were the Jews hiding? And the people who hid the Jews could also be killed for doing so. Why would people take that risk?
2. Katie is having an amazing ride around the Versailles palace grounds while Zack is back at the gate trying to find Butterball's owners. Do you think Zack would rather be out riding? What attitude is he demonstrating?

Chapter 11

1. The Bible tells us, "*A joyful heart makes a cheerful face*" (Proverbs 15:13 NASB). How does Zack demonstrate that after falling in the Versailles canal?
2. Katie tells the Versailles guard that she wasn't on the grass—

when she clearly was. What is something you have struggled with that you know you shouldn't do, but you keep repeating the same wrong actions or words? What do you think Katie (and you) should do?

Chapter 12

1. Katie is learning that "whatever you feed, grows." Explain how "feeding" our new spiritual nature with God's truths from the Bible helps us grow to be more like Jesus.
2. Look back at pages 122 - 124 and then explain in your own words why we can know the Bible is completely trustworthy and reliable in everything it says.

Chapter 13

1. Zack orders coffee, although he's never had it before. Why do you think he does that? What things have you said or done just because other people are doing it? Is that a good reason for deciding what you will do or say? Why?
2. Katie starts to tell the owner of the flower stall that Butterball didn't really wet on the herbs, but suddenly remembers the verse, "*He who is faithful in a very little thing is faithful also in much; and he who is unrighteous in a very little thing is unrighteous also in much*" (Luke 16:10 NASB). How did God's Word make a difference in Katie's actions?

Chapter 14

1. Katie urges André to tell his parents about his desire to play the accordion professionally rather than to take over the family bakery. What do you think André should do? Why?

2. Katie is getting frantic and is afraid they've missed finding Butterball's owners. She says they don't have a choice and must sneak the puppy into the Louvre, but Zack says, "Nothing ever makes lying and cheating okay." Which of them do you think is right? Why?

Chapter 15

1. As Katie and Zack walk around the Louvre, they see amazing artifacts from all over the world. Have you ever been inside a fascinating museum? Where? What did you like the most?
2. What are the consequences of Katie sneaking Butterball into the Louvre? What do you think Katie should learn from this?

Chapter 16

1. Katie reads the verse about how God wants us to have pure hearts and hands and not tell lies (Psalm 24:4). She feels convicted again, and confesses to God her dishonesty of sneaking Butterball into the Louvre. After praying, even though she is still worried about finding Butterball's owners, what difference does she notice in her heart?
2. André said earlier that he would pray for the right time to talk with his parents about his desire to play the accordion professionally. Now in the car he prays again, then tells his parents. What can you learn from André's actions?

Chapter 17

1. Mr. Gateman tells Katie, "Life is always a combination of joys and challenges. That is why spending time in God's Word each day is so important—so you will know *how* to meet those challenges." Romans 12:2 says to "*let God transform you into a new person by changing the way you think.*" How does God use His Word to change us and help us know how to meet life's challenges?

2. Katie finally figures out what important thing she is to learn about her relationship with her Father that will transform her. What is it Katie learns and how can it transform her? And what is the important thing Katie learns about herself? How did she practice that with Zack right away?

Chapter 18

1. Katie had one final "loose end" to take care of. What was it she did?

2. What have you learned from Katie's and Zack's adventure in Paris? How will you practice what you have learned?

Don't forget to get ***30 Days with God*** so you can read it along with Katie and Zack!
Download it for free or purchase it at
www.KatieandZackAdventures.com.
Also available for purchase at www.Amazon.com.

Thanks!

Thanks always to my precious husband, **Stottler**, for *all* you are doing to make these books possible. They wouldn't be happening without your behind-the-scenes work. I love you!!!

Dad, you gave our family such a gift in providing for us and giving us the opportunity to travel. Seeing some other countries as a young girl opened up the world to me. Thank you so much!

Frank Marocco, I miss you dearly, and look forward to hearing your astounding accordion in heaven. You brought so much joy to Stottler and me. Thanks for your patience as a teacher and your genuine friendship. Thanks too, **Anne**, for your continued friendship and for keeping us a part of the Marocco family.

Thanks a million, **Didier Heslon**, for taking the time to read the manuscript and for giving me your insights into the French way of life. You have answered countless questions, and I am so grateful. And your help with the French words has been invaluable.

Thanks, **Josh McDowell** for your vital insights on youth culture, and for your encouragement on the Katie & Zack Adventure Series. And **Dottie**, thank you so much for your enthusiasm for these books. I love and appreciate you both so much!

Marilyn Mitchell, thank you for helping this born-and-bred cowgirl with all the English riding terms. And thanks, **Ilene Bradberry**, for introducing us.

I'm very grateful to **James and Lisa Bryant** for your help with "Aussie speech," (even though I'm going to have to use it in a later book). Thanks for your wisdom from the other side of the hemisphere!

Erin Pollock, you have been so gracious and kind to help me with all sorts of projects for these books! Thank you, thank you, thank you!

Peter Antosh, **Donna Bahler**, and **Nan Green**, along with Didier—I really needed your help with all those French words, and you guys have been wonderful! How crazy for someone who only speaks a bit of Spanish and Italian to decide to do a book in France. ☺ But you made it possible. Thank you!

Always great appreciation to my proofers: Stottler, **Bonnie Lang**, **Betty Freeze**, and Nan Green, as well as eternal thanks to my fabulous editor, **Barb Lilland**, and my internal designer, **Beth Vander Meulen**. I depend on you all greatly!

And a *special* thanks to **Chris Beatrice** for this incredible cover and the unbelievably adorable puppy above the chapters. Way to go, Chris!

Thanks again, **Abigail** and **Elsa Schweizer** and **Oliver Schumacher** for giving more of your time to pose for pictures. You have brought Katie and Zack to life over and over again. And thank you, **Nate Heslon**, for your pictures, too.

Last but not least, a special thanks to all my wonderful field testers for giving me your input on the Bible study, *30 Days with God*: **Rachel Compton**, **Meghan Currey**, **Evie Griffin**, **Hannah Kolb**, **Emma Liebelt**, **Abigail** and **Titus** and **Luke Rehard**, and **Quinn Stout**. And **Jeanie Euler**, your insights as a teacher have been invaluable. Thanks to you all!!!

<u>Books in the Katie & Zack Adventure Series:</u>

Adventure at Cassidy Ranch

Adventure in the Bahamas

Adventure in Paris

Adventure in the Wild West (watch for it!)